PENGUIN CLASSICS
Félicie

'I love reading Simenon. He makes me think of Chekhov'
— William Faulkner

'A truly wonderful writer . . . marvellously readable – lucid, simple, absolutely in tune with the world he creates'
— Muriel Spark

'Few writers have ever conveyed with such a sure touch, the bleakness of human life'
— A. N. Wilson

'One of the greatest writers of the twentieth century . . . Simenon was unequalled at making us look inside, though the ability was masked by his brilliance at absorbing us obsessively in his stories'
— *Guardian*

'A novelist who entered his fictional world as if he were part of it'
— Peter Ackroyd

'The greatest of all, the most genuine novelist we have had in literature'
— André Gide

'Superb . . . The most addictive of writers . . . A unique teller of tales'
— *Observer*

'The mysteries of the human personality are revealed in all their disconcerting complexity'
— Anita Brookner

'A writer who, more than any other crime novelist, combined a high literary reputation with popular appeal' – P. D. James

'A supreme writer . . . Unforgettable vividness' – *Independent*

'Compelling, remorseless, brilliant'
— John Gray

'Extraordinary masterpieces of the twentieth century'
— John Banville

Georges Simenon was born on 12 February 1903 in Liège, Belgium, and died in 1989 in Lausanne, Switzerland, where he had lived for the latter part of his life. Between 1931 and 1972 he published seventy-five novels and twenty-eight short stories featuring Inspector Maigret.

Simenon always resisted identifying himself with his famous literary character, but acknowledged that they shared an important characteristic:

> My motto, to the extent that I have one, has been noted often enough, and I've always conformed to it. It's the one I've given to old Maigret, who resembles me in certain points . . . 'understand and judge not'.

Penguin is publishing the entire series of Maigret novels.

GEORGES SIMENON

Félicie

Translated by DAVID COWARD

PENGUIN BOOKS

PENGUIN CLASSICS

UK | USA | Canada | Ireland | Australia
India | New Zealand | South Africa

Penguin Books is part of the Penguin Random House group of companies
whose addresses can be found at global.penguinrandomhouse.com.

First published in French as *Félicie est là* by Éditions Gallimard 1944
This translation first published 2015

011

Copyright 1944 by Georges Simenon Limited
Translation copyright © David Coward, 2015
GEORGES SIMENON ® Simenon.tm
MAIGRET ® Georges Simenon Limited
All rights reserved

The moral rights of the author and translator have been asserted

Set in Dante MT Std 12.5/15 pt
Typeset by Palimpsest Book Production Limited, Falkirk, Stirlingshire
Printed and bound in Great Britain by Clays Ltd, Elcograf S.p.A.

ISBN: 978-0-241-18866-8

www.greenpenguin.co.uk

MIX
Paper from
responsible sources
FSC® C018179

Penguin Random House is committed to a
sustainable future for our business, our readers
and our planet. This book is made from Forest
Stewardship Council® certified paper.

Contents

1. *Pegleg's Funeral*

It was a quite extraordinary moment, in that it probably lasted for no more than a second, but it was like those dreams which, people say, seem to go on for a long, long time. Years later, Maigret could still have pointed out the exact spot where it had happened, the part of the pavement on which his feet had been standing, the very flagstone on which his shadow had fallen; he could not only have reconstituted the smallest details of the scene, but also recalled the wafted smells and the vibrations of the air which had the feel of a childhood memory.

It was the first time that year that he'd gone out without an overcoat, the first time he'd been in the country at ten in the morning. Even his large pipe tasted of springtime. It was still chilly. Maigret walked heavily, hands in his trouser pockets. Félicie walked by his side, just a little in front of him, having to take two quick steps to his one.

They were both walking past the front of a new shop built of pink brick. In the window were a few vegetables, two or three kinds of cheese and a selection of sausages in an earthenware dish.

Félicie put on a spurt, stretched out one arm, pushed open a glazed door, and it was then, sparked off by the bell which was set ringing, that it happened.

Now, this shop doorbell was no ordinary doorbell. Metal

tubes dangled behind the door. When the door opened, the tubes knocked against each other and began to chime, making light, ethereal music.

Long ago, when Maigret was a boy, there had been a pork-butcher in his village who had had his shop completely refurbished. It had a set of chimes just like these.

That is why that moment seemed to hang suspended. For a time whose length was impossible to determine, Maigret was transported out of the living present and saw his surroundings as though he were not inside the skin of the thick-set detective chief inspector whom Félicie had in tow.

It was as if the boy he had once been was hiding somewhere, invisible, looking on with a strong urge to burst out laughing.

Get a grip! What was this solemn, bulky adult doing in a place which was as insubstantial as a child's toy, following Félicie, who was wearing a ridiculous red hat that looked straight out of the pages of a children's picture book?

An investigation? Was he looking into a murder? Hunting down the perpetrator? And doing so while the little birds chirruped and the grass was an innocent green and the bricks as pink as Turkish delight and there were new flowers everywhere and even the leeks in the window looked like flowers?

Yes, he would remember this moment later and not always fondly. For years and years, it was a tradition at Quai des Orfèvres, on certain frisky spring mornings, to call out to Maigret with heavy sarcasm:

'Oh, Maigret . . .'

'What?'

'Félicie's here!'

And in his mind's eye he would see that slim figure in the striking clothes, those wide eyes the colour of forget-me-not, the pert nose and especially the hat, that giddy, crimson bonnet perched on the top of her head with a bronze-green feather shaped like a blade stuck in it.

'*Félicie's here!*'

A growl. Everyone knew that Maigret always began growling like a bear whenever anyone reminded him of Félicie, who had given him more trouble than all the 'hard' men who had been put behind bars courtesy of the inspector.

That May morning, standing in the doorway of the shop, Félicie was all too real. Above the transparent advertising stickers for starch and metal polish was written, in yellow letters, *Mélanie Chochoi, Groceries*. Félicie waited until the inspector decided to emerge from his daydream.

Finally he took one step forwards, found himself in the real world once more and picked up the thread of his investigation into the murder of Jules Lapie, also known as Pegleg.

Her features sharp and aggressively sarcastic, Félicie waited for his questions as she had been doing all morning. Behind the counter, a short, motherly woman, Mélanie Chochoi, hands crossed over her ample stomach, gazed at the strange couple formed by the detective chief inspector of the Police Judiciaire and Pegleg's housekeeper.

Maigret was drawing gently on his pipe, looking around him at the brown racks full of tinned foods and then, through the shop window, out at the unfinished road, where the recently planted saplings were still no more than the frail offspring of trees. Taking his watch from his pocket, he spoke at last:

'You came in here at quarter past ten, you said. That's correct, isn't it? How can you be sure that was the exact time?'

A thin, scornful smile parted Félicie's lips.

'Come and see for yourself,' she said.

When he was standing next to her, she pointed to the back of the shop, which was Mélanie Chochoi's kitchen. In the semi-darkness could be seen a rattan chair on which a marmalade cat had rolled itself into a ball on a red cushion; just above it, on a shelf, an alarm clock registered 10.17.

Félicie was right. She was always right. The grocer was wondering what these people had come to her shop for.

'What did you buy?'

'A pound of butter . . . Would you get me a pound of butter, Madame Chochoi? The inspector here wants me to do exactly what I did the day before yesterday. Slightly salted, wasn't it? . . . Wait . . . You can also give me a packet of peppercorns, a tin of tomatoes and two loin chops . . .'

Everything was strange in the world which Maigret inhabited that morning, and it required an effort on his part to convince himself that he was not some sort of giant floundering through a toy construction set.

A few kilometres out of Paris, he had turned his back on the banks of the Seine. At Poissy he had climbed the slope and suddenly, surrounded by the reality of fields and orchards, he had discovered this remote world whose existence was signalled by a signboard on the side of a new road: Jeanneville Village.

A few years earlier there would have been the same fields, the same meadows, the same groves of trees here as elsewhere. Then a man of business had come this way, with a wife or mistress named Jeanne no doubt, hence the name Jeanneville which had been given to this world in gestation.

Roads had been laid out and avenues planted with still uncertain saplings, their thin trunks wrapped in straw to protect them from the cold.

Villas and houses had been built willy-nilly. It did not amount either to a village or a town, it was a universe apart, incomplete, with gaps between the buildings, wooden fences, areas of waste-ground, ridiculously useless gas-lamps on streets which were still only names on blue signs:

'My Dream' . . . 'The Last Lap' . . . 'Dunrentin' . . . each poky house had its name inscribed in a decorated plaque, and lower down the hill were Poissy, the silver ribbon of the Seine, where all too real barges plied, and railway tracks on which real trains ran. Further along the plateau, farms could be seen, and the steeple at Orgeval.

But here the only manifestation of true reality was the old woman who ran the grocery, Mélanie Chochoi, who had been uprooted by the developers from a neighbouring town and given a fine, brand-new shop so that buying and selling would not be entirely absent from this new universe.

'Anything else, dear?'

'Wait a minute . . . What else did I buy on Monday?'

'Hairpins.'

Mélanie's shop sold everything: toothbrushes, face-powder, paraffin, picture postcards . . .

'I think that's all, isn't it?'

From the shop, as Maigret had already checked, Pegleg's house could not be seen, nor the path that ran round the outside of the garden.

'The milk!' said Félicie, remembering. 'I was forgetting the milk!'

She explained to the inspector, still with that air of sovereign disdain:

'You've been asking so many questions that I almost forgot my jug of milk . . . Anyway, I had it on Monday. I left it in the kitchen. A blue jug with white dots, you'll see it next to the butagaz stove. Isn't that so, Madame Chochoi?'

Every time she supplied any piece of information, she did so in a loud voice, like Caesar's wife who must be above suspicion.

She's the one who insists that nothing should be overlooked.

'And what did I tell you last Monday, Madame Chochoi?'

'I do believe you said my Zouzon's got worms, seeing as how he's always swallowing his fur . . .'

Zouzon was obviously the tomcat snoozing on the red cushion on the chair.

'Wait a sec . . . You took your *Ciné-Journal* and one of them twenty-five sou novels.'

At one end of the counter was a display of the gaudy covers of popular magazines and books, but Félicie did not even give them a second glance and just shrugged her shoulders.

'How much do I owe you? Please hurry, because the inspector insists that everything should happen the way it did on Monday, and I didn't stay here this long then.'

Maigret broke in:

'Tell me, Madame Chochoi, since we're talking about Monday morning . . . When you were serving this young lady, did you happen to hear the sound of a car?'

The grocer stares out at the sunlit landscape through the window.

'I couldn't rightly say . . . Wait a bit . . . It isn't as if we get a great many cars round here. You just hear them passing by on the main road . . . What day was it? . . . I can remember a small red car which drove past behind the house where the Sébiles live. But as to saying what day that was . . .'

Just in case, Maigret jotted down in his notebook: *Red Car, Sébile*.

Then he was outside again with Félicie, who swayed her hips as she walked and wore her coat over her shoulders like a cape, leaving the sleeves trailing loosely behind her.

'This way. When I go home, I always take this short cut.'

A narrow path between kitchen gardens.

'Did you meet anyone?'

'Wait. You'll see.'

He saw. She was right. As they joined a new, wider path, the postman, who had just come up the hill, passed them on his bike, turned to them and cried:

'Nothing for you, Mademoiselle Félicie!'

She eyed Maigret:

'He saw me here on Monday, at the same time, just like almost every morning.'

They skirted an appallingly ugly house covered with sky-blue stucco and set in a garden filled with lifeless earthenware animals then walked along a hedge. Félicie pushed open the side-gate. Her trailing coat brushed against a row of redcurrant bushes.

'Here we are. This is the garden. You'll see the arbour in a moment.'

They had left the house at a few minutes before ten by the other door, which opened on to a wide avenue. To get to the shop and come back they had described almost a full circle. They walked past a border of carnations, which would soon flower, and beds of young salad plants of a delicate green colour.

'*He* should have been here . . .' Félicie said sternly, pointing to a tightly drawn string and a dibble pushed firmly into the earth. '*He* had started pricking out his tomatoes. The row is half finished. When *he* failed to appear, I assumed *he* had gone off for a glass of rosé . . .'

'Did he drink a lot of that?'

'When he was thirsty. You'll find his glass upside down on the barrel in the wine store.'

The garden of a careful man with a modest private income, the kind of a house that thousands of hard-pressed citizens dream of building, where they might spend their declining years. They moved out of the sunlight and stepped into the bluish shade of the yard, which was a continuation of the garden. There was an arbour on the right. On the table in the arbour was a small decanter containing some strong spirit and a glass with a thick bottom.

'You saw the bottle and the glass. Now this morning you told me your employer never drank spirits when he was by himself, and especially not what's in that decanter.'

She gives him a defiant look. She seems to be constantly presenting him, and not by accident, with a sight of the clear blue of her irises, so that he can see in them for himself a confirmation of her total innocence.

Even so, she retorts: 'He was only my employer.'

'I know. You already told me.'

Good God! How irritating it is to have to deal with someone like Félicie! What else has she said in that shrill voice which grates of Maigret's nerves? Oh yes, she said:

'It's not my business to reveal secrets which are not mine to tell. To some people I may have been just his live-in housekeeper. But that was not how he saw me, and one day people will discover that . . .'

'Discover what?'

'Oh nothing!'

'Are you implying that you were sleeping with Pegleg?'

'What do you take me for?'

Taking a risk, Maigret asks:

'His daughter, then?'

'It's no good questioning me. One day, perhaps . . .'

That was Félicie for you! Stiff as an ironing board, acid-tongued, capricious, a sharp face badly daubed with powder and lipstick, a little housemaid who puts on airs at a Sunday dance, and then suddenly an unnerving beadiness appears in her eye, or maybe something resembling a distant smile of contemptuous irony crosses her lips.

'If he had a drink when he was by himself, it was no business of mine.'

In fact, old Jules Lapie, usually known as Pegleg, had not had a drink by himself. Of that Maigret is quite certain. A man who works in his garden, with his straw hat on his head and clogs on his feet, does not suddenly abandon his tomato seedlings, bring out the decanter of old brandy from the sideboard and pour himself a glass in the arbour.

At some point, on this green-painted table, there had been another glass. Someone has removed it. Was it Félicie?

'What did you do when you didn't see Lapie?'

'Nothing. I went into the kitchen, lit the gas to boil the milk and drew water from the pump to wash the vegetables.'

'After that?'

'I stood on the old chair and changed the fly-paper.'

'Still with your hat on? Because you wear a hat when you go shopping, don't you?'

'I'm no scullery maid.'

'When did you take your hat off?'

'When I took the milk pan off the stove. I went up . . .'

Everything is brand new and fresh in the house, which the old man christened 'Cape Horn'. The staircase smells of varnished pine. The treads creak.

'So go up. I'll follow you.'

She pushes open the door to her bedroom, where a

box-mattress covered with flowered cretonne serves as a divan and photos of film stars grace the walls.

'So, I take off my hat. Then I think, "Drat! I forgot to open the window in Monsieur Jules' room."

'I walk across the landing . . . I open the door and I scream . . .'

Maigret is still drawing smoke from his pipe, which he had refilled as he was crossing the garden. He studies a chalked shape on the polished floor, the outline of Pegleg's body in the position it was in when it was discovered on Monday morning.

'And the revolver?' he asks.

'There was no revolver. You know that because you've read the report by the local police.'

Above the mantelpiece is a scale model of a three-masted ship, and on the walls are a number of paintings all of sailing vessels. It is like being in the house of an old, retired seafaring man, but the police lieutenant who conducted the original investigation has told Maigret all about Pegleg's strange adventure.

Jules Lapie was never a sailor but a book-keeper with a firm of ship's chandlers at Fécamp supplying nautical equipment – sails, ropes, pulleys – as well as provisions for long sea voyages.

A thick-set bachelor, meticulous in his habits, maybe obsessively so, with a generally grizzled air and a brother who is a ship's carpenter.

One morning. Jules Lapie, then aged about forty, goes aboard the *Sainte-Thérèse*, a three-master which is sailing that same day for Chile, where it will take on a cargo of phosphates. Lapie is given the humdrum job of ensuring that all the merchandise ordered has been delivered and of collecting payment from the captain.

What happens next? The Fécamp matelots are all too ready to have a laugh at the fastidious book-keeper's expense. He always appears so ill at ease whenever his work takes him on board a ship. Glasses are raised, as is the custom. They make him drink. God knows how much they made him drink to get him so drunk.

However that may be, when with the high tide the *Sainte-Thérèse* glides between the piers of the Normandy port and heads out into the open sea, Jules Lapie, dead to the world, is snoring in a corner of the hold while everyone believes he has gone ashore – at least that is what everyone will say later.

The hatches have been battened down. It is only after two days that the book-keeper is found. The captain refuses to put about and be diverted from his course, and that is how Lapie, who at that time still has both legs, finds himself on the way to Cape Horn.

The adventure will cost him a leg, one day when there's a sudden squall and he falls through an open hatch.

Years later, he will be killed by a single shot from a revolver one Monday in springtime, a few minutes after leaving his tomato seedlings to themselves, while Félicie goes shopping in Mélanie Chochoi's brand-new store.

'Let's go back downstairs,' sighs Maigret.

The house is so quiet, so pleasant because it is as clean as a new pin and filled with nice smells. To the right, the dining room has been turned into a funeral parlour. The inspector opens the door a little into the semi-dark interior, where the shutters are closed and only thin slats of light squeeze into the room. The coffin has been laid on the table, over which a sheet has been spread, and by its side is a hors d'œuvre dish filled with holy water in which a sprig of box tree is soaking.

Félicie waits in the doorway to the kitchen.

'In short, you know nothing, you saw nothing, you have no thoughts whatsoever about the visitor who might have called on your . . . employer – let's just say Jules Lapie – when you were out . . .'

She holds his gaze but does not reply.

'And you are sure that when you got back there was only one glass on the table in the garden?'

'I only saw one. Now, if you can see two . . .'

'Did Lapie get many visitors?'

Maigret sits down next to the butane gas stove and would not say no to a glass of something, preferably of the rosé Félicie mentioned, the barrel of which he has glimpsed in the cool darkness of the wine store. The sun is rising in the sky and steadily drawing up the morning dampness.

'He didn't like visitors.'

A strange man whose life must have been turned inside out by his journey round Cape Horn! Back in Fécamp where, despite his wooden leg, people could not help smiling at his adventure, he keeps more to himself than ever and begins a long legal battle with the owners of the *Sainte-Thérèse*. A battle which he would win by sheer persistence.

He claims the company is at fault, that he was kept on board against his will and that consequently the owners are responsible for his accident. He sets the highest value on the loss of his leg and in court judgement is given in his favour, recognizing his right to sizeable compensation.

The people of Fécamp find it all amusing. He avoids them; he also moves away from the sea, which he loathes, and is one of the first to be seduced by the glossy prospectus put out by the creators of Jeanneville.

Needing a servant, he sends for a young woman he knew as a girl in Fécamp.

'How long have you been living here with him?'

'Seven years.'

'You are twenty-four now. So you were seventeen when . . .'

He allows his thoughts to wander, then suddenly asks:

'Do you have a boyfriend?'

She looks at him without replying.

'I asked if you have a boyfriend.'

'My private life is my business.'

'Does he come here?'

'I don't have to answer that.'

Dammit, he could box her ears for her! There are moments when Maigret feels like swatting her or taking her by the shoulders and giving her a good shake.

'No matter, I'll find out in the end . . .'

'You won't find out anything.'

'Oh, so I won't find out anything . . .'

He stops himself. This is too silly for words! Is he going to stand here arguing with this girl?

'You're sure there isn't anything you want to tell me? Think hard, while there's still time.'

'I've thought about it.'

'You're not hiding anything?'

'I'd be surprised if I had anything left to hide. They say you're very clever at making people talk!'

'Well, we'll see.'

'You've seen everything!'

'What do you think you'll do when the family comes and Jules Lapie has been laid to rest?'

'No idea.'

'Would you want to stay on here?'

'Maybe.'

'Do you think you'll be left anything?'

'Very possibly.'

Maigret does not entirely succeed in keeping his temper.

'Be that as it may, my girl, there's one thing I must ask you to remember. As long as the investigation remains ongoing, you are not to leave without first informing the police.'

'So I am not allowed to move out of the house?'

'No!'

'What if I wanted to go away somewhere else?'

'You'll have to ask for my authorization.'

'Do you think I killed him?'

'I'll think whatever I like, and that is none of your business!'

He has had enough. He is furious. He is angry with himself for allowing himself to be reduced to such a state by a kid named Félicie. Twenty-four years old? Come off it! She's a kid of twelve or thirteen who is playing God only knows what sort of games and takes herself very seriously.

'Goodbye!'

'Goodbye!'

'By the way, how will you manage for food?'

'Don't you worry about me! I won't let myself starve to death.'

He is sure she won't. He can imagine her, after he's gone, sitting down at the table in the kitchen and slowly eating whatever there is while she reads one of those cheap novels she buys from Madame Chochoi.

Maigret is incandescent. He has been taken for a ride, in front of everybody, and worse, taken for a ride by that poisonous creature, Félicie.

It is now Thursday. Lapie's family have arrived: his brother Ernest, the ship's carpenter from Fécamp, a rough sort of man with hair cropped short and a face pitted with scars left by small-pox; his wife, who is very fat and has a moustache; their two children, whom she herds before her the way geese are driven in fields; then a nephew, a young man of nineteen, Jacques Pétillon by name, who has come from Paris, feverish and rather sickly, and is regarded with suspicion by the Lapie tribe.

There is as yet no cemetery at Jeanneville. The funeral cortege winds its way to Orgeval, in whose parish the new development lies. The great talking point of the day is the crepe veil worn by Félicie. Where on earth did she find it? It is only later that Maigret learns that she borrowed it from Madame Chochoi.

Félicie does not wait to be shown to her place but takes it, at the head of the procession. She walks in front of the family, ramrod straight, a perfect image of grief, dabbing her eyes with a black-edged handkerchief, also probably on loan from Mélanie, which she has sprinkled liberally with cheap perfume.

Sergeant Lucas, who has spent the night at Jeanneville, is present alongside Maigret. Both follow the cortege along a dusty lane. Larks sing in the clear air.

'She knows something, it's obvious. No matter how clever she thinks she is, she'll trip herself up in the end.'

Lucas agrees. The doors of the small church remain open during the prayer of absolution, so that the atmosphere inside smells more of spring than of incense. It is not very far to the graveside.

After the service is over, the family has to return to the house for the reading of the will.

'Why would my brother have made a will?' says an astonished Ernest Lapie. 'It's not the custom in our family.'

'According to Félicie . . .'

'Félicie! Félicie! It's always Félicie . . .'

Shoulders are shrugged helplessly.

She brazenly edges to the front and manages to be first to throw a shovelful of earth down on to the coffin. Then she turns away tearfully and walks off so quickly that it seems inevitable that she will trip over.

'Don't let her out of your sight, Lucas.'

She walks on, without stopping, through the streets and back lanes of Orgeval. Then suddenly Lucas, who is barely fifty metres behind her, emerges too late into an almost completely empty road, at the end of which a van is vanishing around a corner.

He opens the door of an inn.

'Tell me . . . That van which has just driven off . . .'

'Van? It belongs to Louvet, the garage mechanic. He was here a minute ago, having a drink.'

'Did he give anyone a lift?'

'Don't know . . . Don't think so . . . I haven't been outside . . .'

'Do you know where he'd be going?'

'Paris, like he does every Thursday.'

Lucas hurries off to the post office, which, fortunately for him, is just across the road.

'Hello? . . . Yes . . . It's Lucas . . . Hurry . . . A van, pretty beat up . . . Wait a second . . .'

He turns to the woman behind the counter.

'Do you know the registration number of the van belonging to Monsieur Louvet, the mechanic?'

'Sorry . . . All I can remember is that it ends with an eight . . .'

'Are you still there? . . . Registration number ends in eight . . . A young woman wearing mourning clothes . . . Hello? . . . Don't cut us off . . . No . . . I don't think there's any need to arrest her . . . Just put a tail on her . . . Got that? . . . The chief will phone you himself.'

He rejoins Maigret, who is walking by himself behind the family along the lane which leads from Orgeval to Jeanneville.

'She's gone . . .'

'What?'

'She must have got into the van as it was setting off. I just had time to see it disappear round the corner. I phoned Quai des Orfèvres. They are alerting all divisions. They'll watch the main roads into Paris.'

So, Félicie has gone! Simply, in the full light of day, under the eyes and noses so to speak of Maigret and his best sergeant! Vanished, despite that enormous mourning veil which would make her recognizable from a kilometre away!

Members of the family who turn round from time to time to look back at the two policemen are amazed to see no trace of Félicie. She has taken the front-door key with her. They have to get into the house by going through the garden. Maigret raises the blinds in the dining room, where the bed sheet and the sprig of box are still on the table and an after-smell of candle hangs in the air.

'I could do with a drink,' sighs Ernest Lapie. 'Étienne! Julie! Stop running across those flower beds! There must be some wine here somewhere.'

'In the wine store,' Maigret tells him.

Lapie's wife walks round to Mélanie's to buy cakes for the children and, since she's there, decides to bring some back for everybody.

'There's no reason, inspector, why my brother should have made a will. I know he was a strange character. He kept himself to himself and we didn't have much to do with him any more. But that doesn't mean ...'

Maigret rummages through the drawers of a small desk in one corner of the room. From it he takes out bundles of old bills, carefully classified, and then an old note-case with a grey bloom on it which contains a single brown envelope.

To be opened after my death

'Well, gentlemen, I think this is what we're looking for.'

I, the undersigned, Jules Lapie, being of sound mind and body, in the presence of Ernest Forrentin and François Lepape, both residing in Jeanneville in the commune of Orgeval . . .

Maigret reads in a voice which grows increasingly solemn.

'So Félicie was right!' he said finally. 'She inherits the house and all its contents.'

The family are all dumbstruck. The will contains one brief phrase which they are unlikely to forget:

Given the attitude which my brother and his wife chose to adopt after my accident . . .

'I only told him that it was ridiculous to go stirring heaven and earth just because . . .' comments Ernest Lapie.

Given the conduct of my nephew, Jacques Pétillon . . .

The young man who has come from Paris looks like the class dunce on speech-day.

None of it matters. Félicie has inherited everything. And Félicie, God only know why, has disappeared.

2. Six O'Clock on the Métro

Maigret, his hands thrust in his trouser pockets, has halted in the hall in front of the bamboo coat stand in the middle of which is a mirror shaped like a diamond. He peers into it and sees a face that would normally make most people laugh, for it looks like the face of a child who wants something but is too shy to ask for it. But Maigret is not laughing. He reaches out, takes the broad-brimmed straw hat which is hanging on one of the hooks and puts it on.

Well! Old Pegleg's head was even bigger than that of the inspector, who regularly has to trail round several hat shops before finding one to fit him. It sets him thinking. With the straw hat still on his head, he returns to the dining room to take another look at the photo of Jules Lapie that was found in the drawer.

Once, when a foreign criminologist was asking the commissioner of the Police Judiciaire about Maigret's working methods, he replied with an enigmatic smile:

'Maigret? What can I say? He just settles into an investigation the way a man gets into a pair of slippers.'

Today, it is almost the case that the inspector gets into, if not the victim's slippers, then at least his clogs. For there they are, just by the door, on the right, in a place which is quite clearly theirs. In fact everything is in its place. If it wasn't for the fact that Félicie was not there, Maigret might well think that life in the house is going on just as it did in the past, that he is Lapie, that he will now walk at his own slow pace towards the vegetable patch to finish pricking out the row of tomato seedlings.

The sun is setting in splendour behind the light-coloured houses that can be seen from the garden. Ernest Lapie, the dead man's brother, has declared that he intends to spend the night at Poissy and has sent the rest of the family back to Fécamp. The others – the neighbours and a few farm-workers from Orgeval who followed the hearse – must either have gone home or else are in the Anneau d'Or, having a drink.

Sergeant Lucas is there too, because Maigret has told him to take his travel bag there and stay in touch with Paris by phone.

Pegleg had a large head, a square face, grey eyebrows and grey whiskers all over his face which he shaved just once a week. He was mean with money. You only had to cast an eye over his accounts. It was obvious that for him every sou counted. Had his brother not admitted it?

'Of course, he was very *near* . . .'

And when one Norman says of another Norman that he is *near* . . .

The weather is mild. The sky is changing perceptibly to purple. Cool breezes blow in from the fields, and Maigret catches himself, pipe in mouth, standing there with a slight stoop, the way Lapie used to stand. It even gets to the point where, as he makes his way to the wine store, he drags his left leg. He turns the spigot on the barrel of rosé, rinses the glass and fills it . . . At this time of day, Félicie would normally be in the kitchen and probably the smell of her ragout would have floated out into the garden. It is watering time too. People can be seen watering in the gardens round about. Dusk invades the Cape Horn, where, when the old man was alive, the lights would not be turned on until the very last minute.

Why was he killed? Maigret cannot help thinking that one day he will himself be retired. He too will have a small house in the country, a garden, a large straw hat . . .

Pegleg would not have been killed in the course of a burglary because, according to his brother, he had virtually no assets outside his famous settlement. A savings pass-book had been found, plus two thousand francs in notes in an envelope and a few municipal bonds issued by the City of Paris. They had also found his gold watch.

Right, that means looking elsewhere. Maigret will have to dig himself deeper under the man's skin. He is surly, churlish, taciturn and finicky. He is a loner. The slightest disturbance to his routine certainly makes him angry. He has never thought of marriage, of children, and there is no evidence that he was a philanderer.

What was Félicie trying to imply? It was out of the question! Félicie was lying! Lying comes as easily to her as breathing! Or rather, she makes up truths to suit her purposes. It would be too simple, too banal for her to be just a servant in the old man's house. She would rather let it be thought that if he had sent for her . . .

Maigret turns and looks at the kitchen window. What had been the relationship between these two people living in such isolation? He has a feeling, no, he is sure that they must have squabbled like cat and dog.

Suddenly, Maigret gives a start. He has just emerged from the wine store, where he has drunk a second glass of wine. He is standing there in the twilight with the straw hat on his head and wonders for a moment if he is not dreaming. An electric light bulb has just been switched on behind the kitchen's lacy curtains. He can see gleaming saucepans hanging on the gloss-painted walls, he hears the 'pfft' as the gas stove is lit. By the inspector's watch it is ten minutes to eight.

He opens the door and sees Félicie, who has already hung her hat and the veil on a peg on the hallstand and has just put a pan of water on to boil.

'Hello! You've come back then?'

She is not startled, she just looks at him all the way from his feet to his head, and her eyes settle on the straw hat, which Maigret has completely forgotten.

He sits down. He must automatically have chosen the old man's chair by the window and now, as he stretches out his legs, Félicie comes and goes as if he is not there, lays the table for her dinner and fetches the butter, bread and cured sausage from the cupboard.

'Tell me, my girl . . .'

'I'm not your girl.'

'Tell me, Félicie . . .'

'Say mademoiselle!'

Good God! What an unpleasant creature the girl is! Maigret feels the same annoyance that you feel when you try to pick up a small animal which keeps slipping through your fingers, a lizard for example, or a snake. He is uneasy about taking her seriously but he has no choice for he senses that it is from her and her alone that he will learn the truth.

'I asked you not to leave.'

She breaks into a smug smile, as if to say: 'But I left anyway! So there!'

'May I ask why you went to Paris?'

'For the ride!'

'Really? Bear in mind that I shall soon know every last detail of where you went and what you did.'

'I know. A moron followed me everywhere.'

'What moron?'

'A tall red-headed moron who dogged my footsteps on six separate trains on the Métro.'

Inspector Janvier most likely, who must have been sent to tail her from the moment the mechanic's van arrived at Porte Maillot.

'Whom did you go to see?'

'Nobody.'

She sits down to eat, then goes one better. She props up one of her cheap novels in front of her. She has kept her page with a knife and calmly begins to read.

'Tell me, Félicie . . .'

The obstinacy of a goat, that's what struck the inspector the moment he saw her again. It is only now that he realizes it. Head held high and stubborn as a goat, she is grimly ready to charge anything that looks like an obstacle.

'Do you intend to spend tonight alone in this house?'

'What about you? Are you thinking of staying here?'

She eats, she reads. He hides his irritation under a veil of irony that he hopes will sound paternal.

'You told me this morning that you were certain you would inherit . . .'

'And . . . ?'

'How did you know?'

'I just did!'

She has made coffee for herself and pours herself a cup. It is clear she likes coffee; she savours it but doesn't offer any to the inspector. At this point, Maigret gets to his feet with a sigh:

'I will come and see you tomorrow.'

'Please yourself.'

'I hope you will have thought it all over.'

She defies him with a look from those pale eyes, in which he can read nothing. Then, with a shrug of her shoulders, she says casually:

'Thought all what over?'

Outside the front door of Cape Horn, Maigret discovers Inspector Janvier, who has continued shadowing the girl all the way back to Jeanneville. The end of his cigarette glows in the dark. There is no wind. Stars above. The croaking of frogs.

'I recognized her straight away, sir, from the description Lucas phoned through. When the van arrived at the toll point, she was sitting next to the mechanic, and they both seemed to be getting on like a house on fire. She got out. She walked up Avenue de la Grande-Armée, looking in the shop windows. At the corner of Rue Villaret-de-Joyeuse, she went into a cake shop, where she ate half a dozen cream cakes and drank a glass of port.'

'Did she spot you?'

'I don't think so.'

'Well I do.'

Janvier looks embarrassed.

'From there she headed for the Métro. She bought a second-class ticket, and we changed first at Concorde, then again at Saint-Lazare. The carriages were almost empty. She sat and read a novelette which she had in her handbag. In all, we changed trains five times . . .'

'Did she talk to anyone?'

'No. Gradually more and more passengers got on. At six o'clock, when the shops and offices closed, it was the rush hour. You know what it's like . . .'

'Go on.'

'At the Les Ternes station, we were wedged in the crowd less than a metre apart. It was then, I admit, that I realized she knew she was being followed. She stared at me. I had the impression, sir . . . How can I put it . . . For a brief moment, her face was completely different. It was as if she was afraid. I'm certain that for a moment she was afraid of me, or of something . . . It only lasted a few seconds then suddenly she was elbowing her way out and on to the platform . . .'

'Are you quite sure she didn't speak to anybody?'

'Certain. On the platform she waited until the train began to move off and kept her eyes fixed on the crowded carriage.'

'Did she seem to be looking for anyone in particular?'

'I couldn't say. What I can tell you is that her face relaxed, and when the train had disappeared into the dark tunnel she was unable to prevent herself flashing me a look of triumph. Then she went up to street level. She didn't seem to know where she was. She drank an aperitif in the bar on the corner of Avenue des Ternes, then she consulted a rail timetable and took a taxi to Saint-Lazare station . . . That's everything . . . I got the same train as her to Poissy, and we both walked up the hill, one behind the other.'

'Have you eaten?'

'I managed to snatch a sandwich at the station.'

'Stay here and wait till Lucas comes.'

Maigret turns away and walks out of the peaceful village of Jeanneville, where all that can be seen are a few pink lights in windows. He soon reaches Orgeval and locates Lucas in the Anneau d'Or. Lucas is not alone. The man he is with, who wears blue overalls, can only be Louvet, the mechanic, who is in high spirits; the four or five coasters already on the table in front of him show why.

'My boss, Detective Chief Inspector Maigret . . .' says Lucas by way of introduction. He too smells of alcohol.

'As I was saying to the sergeant, sir, I never suspected a thing when I got into the van. I go to Paris every Thursday afternoon to get whatever I haven't got here . . .'

'At the same time?'

'Give or take . . .'

'Did Félicie know?'

'To be honest, I hardly knew her, and then only by sight, because I'd never spoken to her. On the other hand, I knew

Pegleg, who came in here every evening to play cards with Forrentin and Lepape. Sometimes it was the landlord, sometimes me or somebody else who made the fourth hand . . . Look . . . That's Forrentin and Lepape over there, in the corner on the left, with the mayor and the builder.'

'When did you realize there was someone in your vehicle?'

'Just before I got to Saint-Germain. I heard a sort of moaning just behind me. I thought it was the wind, because it was a bit blowy, and it kept lifting the tarpaulin. Then suddenly I hear this voice saying: "Have you got a light?"

'I turn round and I see her. She'd lifted her veil and had a cigarette in her mouth.

'She wasn't laughing, that's for sure. She was dead pale, and the cigarette between her lips was trembling . . .

'"What are you doing there?" I asked.

'Then she started talking, she talked non-stop . . . She said it was absolutely vital for her to get to Paris as soon as possible, how it was a matter of life and death, how the men who killed Pegleg were now after her, that the police didn't have a clue about what was going on.

'I pulled over for a moment so she could sit next to me in front, on the bench-seat, because she'd been squatting on an old box which was none too clean . . .

'"Later . . . later . . ." she kept saying, "when I've done what I have to do maybe I'll tell you all about it. But whatever happens I'll always be grateful to you for saving me."

'Then as soon as we got to the toll-point she thanks me and gets out, very graceful, like a princess.'

Lucas and Maigret exchange glances.

'And now, if it's all right with you, we'll have a last one for the road – no no, my round! – and then I'm going to get something to eat . . . I hope I'll not get into any trouble on account of all this, will I? Cheers . . .'

Ten in the evening. Lucas has gone off to keep Cape Horn under surveillance, replacing Janvier, who has gone back to Paris. The bar of the Anneau d'Or is blue with smoke. Maigret has eaten too much and is now on his third or fourth glass of the local marc-brandy.

As he straddles a straw-bottomed chair, elbows leaning on its back, there are moments when it seems he is nodding off. His eyes are half-closed, and a faint tendril of smoke rises straight up from the bowl of his pipe, while four men play cards on the table in front of him.

As they deal and flip the greasy cards on the garnet-red cloth, they talk, answer questions and sometimes tell an anecdote. The landlord, Monsieur Joseph, is sitting in for old Lapie, and the mechanic has come back after eating his dinner.

'In a word, then,' murmurs Maigret, 'he was on to a good thing. A bit like some respectable country priest with his housekeeper. He probably made sure he got his home comforts and . . .'

Lepape, who is deputy mayor of Orgeval, winks at the others. His partner, Forrentin, is manager of the Jeanneville development and lives in the best house, on the main road, just by the hoarding which informs all who pass by that there are still plots for sale in Jeanneville.

'A priest and his housekeeper, eh?' grins the deputy mayor.

Forrentin just gives a sardonic smile.

'Get on with you! It's obvious you didn't know him,' explains the landlord, declaring belote with three cards of the same suit. 'Dead he may be, but you can't deny he was the sorest bear's head you ever did see . . .'

'What do you mean, sorest bear's head?'

'Well, he was always moaning about something or nothing from morning to night. He was never satisfied. Take that business with the glasses . . .'

He turns to the others to back him up.

'First, he said the bottoms of my liqueur glasses were too thick, and he managed to spot an odd glass on the top shelf that suited him better. Then one day as he was decanting from one glass to another, he saw that both contained exactly the same amount and he was hopping mad . . .

'"But you chose that glass yourself," I told him.

'Well! He went into town, bought a glass and brought it back to me. It held a third as much as the ones I use.

'"It doesn't make any difference," I told him. "You'll just have to pay five sous extra."

'After that, he didn't come in here for a week. Then one night I spot him standing in the frame of the door.

'"What about my glass?"

'"Five sous extra," I say.

'Away he goes again. It lasted a month, and in the end I was the one who blinked because we were short of a fourth for cards.

'So can't a man say, yes or no, that he was like a bear with a sore head? He was like that, as near as dammit, with his housekeeper. They were at each other's throats morning to night. You could hear them arguing from miles away. They'd stop talking to each other for weeks on end. I think that actually she always had the last word because, no offence intended, she was even more Norman than he was . . . Anyway, I'd be interested to know who killed the old boy. There was no harm in him really. It's just the way he was. I never saw a game of cards when he didn't reckon at some point that people were trying to cheat him.'

'Did he often go to Paris?' Maigret asks after a moment.

'Next to never. Once a quarter, to collect his pension. He'd go off in the morning and come back the same evening.'

'How about Félicie?'

'Hey, you boys, did Félicie used to go to Paris?'

The others don't really know. On the other hand she was often seen on a Sunday, dancing in a bar which had a band on the river, at Poissy.

'Do you know what old Lapie called her? When he talked about her, he used to say "my cockatoo" on account of her fancy ways of dressing. You see, inspector – our friend Forrentin here is going to be vexed again, but I'm only saying what I think – the people who live in Jeanneville are all more or less crazy. This is not a land where good Christian folk live. They are poor devils who have slaved all their lives and dreamed of retiring to the country one day. Well, the great day arrives! They get taken in by

Forrentin's pretty brochures . . . Don't deny it, Forrentin, everybody knows you're good at putting sugar all over the pill . . . Anyway, they settle into their paradise on earth and then they realize they are bored rigid . . . and it's costing them a hundred francs an hour . . .

'But it's too late. They've invested their nest-egg in it and now they're going to have to enjoy it as best they can or at least fool themselves into thinking they're enjoying it. Some go to law over the branch of a tree that overhangs their garden or a dog that comes and piddles on their begonias. Then there are others . . .'

Maigret is not asleep; if proof be needed, he reaches out with his hand to raise his glass to his lips. But the heat makes him sluggish, and it is very gradually that he slips back into the real world, which he reconstructs step by step, and once more he sees the unfinished streets of Jeanneville, the infant trees, the houses which look like sets of cubes, the over-tended gardens, the pottery animals and the glass globes.

'Didn't anyone ever come to see him?'

It's impossible! It is all too calm, too tidy, too neat. If life here is really as it is portrayed to him, it is not possible that one fine morning, no longer ago than last Monday, Félicie should go off to do her shopping in Madame Chochoi's grocery store, that Pegleg should suddenly abandon his tomato seedlings to fetch the decanter and one glass from the sideboard in the dining room, go to the arbour, where, alone, he drinks brandy kept for special occasions, and then . . .

He was wearing his gardening hat when he went up to

his room with the highly polished wooden floor. What was he going to do in his bedroom?

No one had heard the shot and yet a gun has been fired, at very close range, less than two metres from his chest, according to the experts.

If only the revolver had been recovered, it might have been thought that Pegleg, having become neurasthenic . . .

The deputy mayor looks for a simpler explanation and, while he tots up his score, murmurs as if it is an answer to every question:

'What could you expect? He was an odd character . . .'

Agreed – but he is dead! Someone killed him! And Félicie, who looks as if butter wouldn't melt in her mouth, managed to give the police the slip immediately after the funeral to go to Paris, where she window-shopped as if nothing had happened, ate cream cakes, drank a glass of port and then rode around on the Métro!

'I wonder who'll move into the house . . .'

The card-players talk nineteen to the dozen, and Maigret, who is not listening, hears it only as a vague background hum. He doesn't say that it will be Félicie. His mind wanders. Images surface and disappear. He scarcely has any idea of time and place . . . Images of Félicie who by now must be in bed reading. She isn't afraid of being alone in that house where someone killed her employer . . . Of the brother, Ernest Lapie, who is angry because of the will. He doesn't need money, but it's beyond his understanding that his brother . . .

'. . . the most solidly built house in the whole of the development . . .'

Whose voice is that? Most probably Forrentin's.

'You couldn't want for a pleasanter house. Just big enough so you've got everything you want within easy reach and . . .'

In his mind's eye, Maigret sees the waxed staircase. Say what you like about Félicie, the way she keeps the house clean is exemplary. As Maigret's mother used to say, you could eat off the floor . . .

A door on the right, the old man's bedroom. A door on the left, Félicie's bedroom. Beyond Félicie's bedroom there's another quite large room which is a jumble of furniture . . .

Maigret furrows his brow. You couldn't call it a presentiment exactly, even less an idea. He has a vague feeling that perhaps there's something not quite right there.

'When that young fellow was there . . .' Lepape is saying.

Maigret gives a start.

'Do you mean the nephew?'

'Yes. He lived with his uncle for six months, maybe more, about a year since. He wasn't very strong. Seems he'd been recommended to get some country air, but he couldn't, being always stuck in Paris . . .'

'What room was he in?'

'There you have it. That's the strangest part of it . . .'

Lepape gives a knowing wink. Forrentin is not best pleased. It's clear the manager of the estate doesn't like stories being spread about the development, which he considers to be his own personal domain.

'It doesn't mean a thing,' he protests.

'Maybe it does, maybe it don't, but the old man and

35

Félicie . . . Listen, inspector. You know the house. To the right of the stairs there's only one room, Pegleg's. Opposite there are two, but you have to go through one to get to the other . . . Well, when the young fellow arrived, his uncle gave him his own room, and he moved across the way, that is, on Félicie's side. He had the first room and the girl slept in the second, which meant she had to pass through her employer's bedroom to get to her own or come out of it . . .'

Forrentin objects:

'So it would have been better to put a young man of eighteen next to a young woman?'

'I'm not saying that, I'm not saying that at all,' repeats Lepape with a sly look in his eye. 'I'm not suggesting anything. I'm just saying that the old man was on Félicie's side of the landing while the nephew was shut away on the other. But as to saying that there was anything going on . . .'

Maigret gives that possibility short shrift. Not that he has any illusions about middle-aged or even old men. Anyway, Pegleg was only sixty and still sprightly . . .

No, it simply doesn't correspond to the picture he has formed of him. He feels he is beginning to understand the grouchy loner whose straw hat he tried on just hours ago.

It's not his relationship with Félicie that bothers him. So what exactly is it? This business of the rooms troubles him.

He repeats to himself over and over, like a schoolboy trying to make his lessons stick in his head:

'The nephew on the right . . . by himself . . . The uncle on the left, then Félicie . . .'

Which means the old man has put himself between the pair of them. Did he want to ensure that the two young people did not get together behind his back? Was he trying to prevent Félicie wandering off the straight and narrow? No, because once his nephew had gone he again left her by herself on the other side of the staircase.

'Your deal, *patron!*'

He stands up. He is going up to bed. He is impatient for it to be tomorrow so he can go back up to the construction set village, see the houses glowing pink in the sunshine and look at those three bedrooms . . . And first thing, he'll phone through to Paris and tell Janvier to find out what he can about the young nephew.

Maigret has paid scarcely any attention to him. No one saw him in Jeanneville on the morning the crime was committed. He is tall, thin and shy and hasn't amounted to much good but he doesn't seem cut out to be a murderer.

According to the reports Maigret has received, his mother, Lapie's sister, married a violinist who played in the brasseries in their part of town. He died young. To raise her son, she found a job as cashier in a shop selling fabrics in Rue du Sentier. She also died, two years ago.

A few months after her death, Lapie took the young man in. They did not get on. It was only to be expected. Jacques Pétillon was a musician like his father, and Pegleg was not the sort who could put up with hearing a violin being scraped or a saxophone being blown under his roof.

So now, to earn a crust, Jacques Pétillon works as a saxophonist in a club in Rue Pigalle. He lives in a sixth-floor furnished room in Rue Lepic.

Maigret falls asleep in a feather bed, into which he sinks, and mice dance all night above his head. The place smells pleasantly of the country, of straw, of mildew too, and cows wake him by lowing, the morning bus stops outside the Anneau d'Or, and Maigret breathes in the aroma of coffee with a little drop of something in it.

Now this business of the bedrooms . . . But first phone Janvier . . .

'Hello . . . Rue Lepic . . . Hôtel Beauséjour . . . bye for now . . .'

He trudges up the hill towards Jeanneville, whose roofs seem to grow directly out of vast fields of waving oats. As he plods on in this fashion, a curious change comes over him. He quickens his step, he keeps watching out for the windows of Cape Horn to appear, he . . . Yes, he is eager to catch up with Félicie, already he is picturing her in her kitchen with those sharp features, turning that nanny-goat forehead in his direction, giving him as frosty a reception as possible with an indefinable look from those transparent pupils.

Was he missing her already?

He understands, he senses, he is certain that Pegleg needed his closest enemy as much as the glass of wine he would go into the store room and pour himself, as much as the air he breathed, as the games of cards every evening and his arguments with his partners over a three-card trick or a trump.

From a distance he spots Lucas, who is kicking his heels at the end of the alley. He couldn't have been very warm during the night. Then, through the open window of her room, he makes out dark hair, now held in place by a kind of turban, and a bustling figure giving the bedclothes a good shake. *Someone* has seen him, *someone* has recognized him, *someone* must already be thinking the kind of welcome which that *someone* intends to give him.

He smiles. He can't help it. That's Félicie for you!

3. *Secrets in a Diary*

'Hello? Is that you, sir? . . . It's Janvier . . .'

A sweaty sort of day. It's not just because the weather is stormy that at times Maigret's face breaks out in a faint rash of perspiration and his fingers tremble with impatience. It reminds him of when he was a boy and feeling scared when he found himself in a place where he shouldn't have been, knowing full well that he didn't belong there.

'Where are you?'

'I'm in Rue des Blancs-Manteaux . . . In a watch-maker's shop . . . I'm phoning from there . . . Our guy is in a nasty-looking bistro across the road . . . He looks as if he's waiting for somebody or something . . . He's just finished another glass of spirits . . .'

Then a silence. Maigret knows exactly what the young inspector will say next.

'I'm wondering, chief, if it wouldn't be better if you came back . . .'

It's been going on all morning, and all morning Maigret has been saying no.

'Just carry on as you are. Phone the minute there's anything new.'

He wonders if he might be wrong, if this is really the way he should be conducting the investigation, but he can't bring himself to leave, something is holding him back, though he'd been hard put to say what exactly.

And a very strange case it's turning out to be! Fortunately, the papers aren't interested in the death of Pegleg. He has murmured to himself at least twenty times so far:

'But the old man was murdered!'

As if the crime has taken a back seat, as if he couldn't help being sidetracked by something else – and that something is Félicie!

The landlord of the Anneau d'Or has loaned him a bike. On it, Maigret looks like a performing bear. It allows him to come and go as he pleases, from Orgeval to the village and from the village to Orgeval.

The weather continues fair and bright. It seems impossible to imagine the landscape here other than lit by spring sunshine, with flowers blooming all along low walls and round the edges of vegetable patches, and pensioners gardening and looking up idly as the inspector or Sergeant Lucas, whom Maigret has kept with him, pass by.

Though he doesn't say so, Lucas also thinks that this is a strange kind of investigation. He finds walking up and down outside Cape Horn extremely tedious. What is he actually supposed to be doing? Watching Félicie? All the windows in the house are open. All her movements are visible. She's done her shopping as usual. She knows the sergeant is following her. Is the chief afraid she will disappear again?

Lucas wonders if this is the case but doesn't dare say so to Maigret. Instead, he keeps it to himself and smokes one pipe after another. Every now and then, for want of something better to do, he kicks a stone with the toe of his shoe.

Since that morning, however, the focus of their inquiries seems to have shifted. The first phone call came from Rue Lepic. Maigret, who was sitting outside on the terrace of the inn next to a laurel bush in a green-painted planter, was expecting it.

Maigret has already settled into a routine. He settles into a routine wherever he goes. He has arranged with the woman in the post office that she should call him through the window the minute there is a phone call for him from Paris.

'That you, sir? . . . It's Janvier . . . I'm phoning from a bar on the corner of Rue Lepic . . .'

Maigret pictures the sloping street, women with handcarts selling fruit and vegetables, housewives in slippers, the colourful bustle of Place Blanche and, between two shop fronts, the entrance to the Hôtel Beauséjour, where he had once made inquiries about another case.

'Jacques Pétillon got back home at six this morning, completely done in. He collapsed on to his bed fully dressed. I went to the Pelican, the club where he works. He hadn't shown up there all night. What do I do now?'

'Hang on there . . . Follow him if he goes out.'

Is the nephew really as innocent as he looks? Would it be better if Maigret, instead of hanging around Félicie, concentrated his efforts on him? He can guess that this is what Janvier thinks. And it is this view that Janvier slips into his second phone call:

'Hello . . . It's Janvier . . . Our man has just gone into the tobacconist's in Rue Fontaine . . . He looks washed out . . . He seems nervy, anxious . . . He kept looking over his shoulder as if he was afraid of being followed, but I don't think he spotted me . . .'

So, Pétillon has had only a few hours' sleep and here he is, on the move again. The tobacconist's in Rue Fontaine is used mainly by shady characters.

'What's he doing now?'

'He's not speaking to anyone . . . He's keeping an eye on the door . . . . Looks like he's waiting for someone . . .'

'Carry on.'

Meanwhile, Maigret has received a little more information about old Lapie's nephew. Why did he never manage to work up any interest in the boy who wanted to become a serious performer and has ended up earning just enough to live by playing the saxophone in a Montmartre nightclub?

Pétillon has seen hard times. He has been reduced to working nights loading vegetables in Les Halles. He has not always had enough to eat. Several times he was forced to leave his violin at the pawnshop.

'Don't you think it's odd, chief, that he should have stayed out all night without setting foot in the Pelican and that now . . . You should see him . . . I think it would be good if you saw him for yourself . . . I get the feeling that he's worried sick, that he's scared . . . Maybe if you were here . . .'

But he always gets the same response:

'Carry on as you are!'

In the meantime, Maigret, perched on his bike, shuttles to and fro between the terrace of the Anneau d'Or, where he waits for phone calls, and the pink house, where he calls on Félicie.

He walks into the house, comes and goes and makes himself at home. She pretends to pay no attention to him, gets on with the housework, makes her meals. She has gone shopping every morning at Madame Chochoi's and bought provisions. Sometimes she looks straight at the inspector, but he finds it impossible to read any sort of feeling whatsoever in those eyes.

She's the one Maigret wants to scare. From the start, she has been too sure of herself. It's impossible that this attitude is not concealing something and he watches for the moment when she will eventually weaken.

But the old man was murdered!

It's her, she is the one who occupies all his thoughts, it's her secret he wants to draw out. He has been prowling round the garden. He has been in the wine store five or six times and each time has poured himself a glass of the rosé which has become a habit with him too. He has made a discovery. Dragging a fork through the layer of leaf-mould which has collected under the hedge, he trawled up a liqueur glass, the twin of the one he found on that first day on the table in the arbour. He showed it to Félicie.

'All you need do now is look for fingerprints on it,' she told him disdainfully without being the least disconcerted.

When he went up to the rooms on the first floor, she did not follow. He searched every nook and corner of Lapie's room. He crossed the landing, entered Félicie's room and began opening all the drawers. She must have heard his comings and goings over her head. Had she been afraid?

And still the weather remains ideal: the softness of the air, the scents wafting in on the breeze and the song of birds coming through the open windows.

And then he manages to find the diary at the back of Félicie's wardrobe, among the tangled knot of stockings and underwear. Pegleg had been quite right to call his housekeeper a cockatoo. Even under her day clothes her taste is for colours, aggressive pinks and acid-sharp greens, and for lace inserts as wide as a hand even though they aren't hand made.

To get a reaction out of her, Maigret goes down to the kitchen to run through the pages of her diary for the previous years. Félicie is busy peelings potatoes, which she then drops into a blue enamel bucket:

13 January – Why didn't he come?
15 January – Plead with him.
19 January – Tormented by uncertainty. Is she his wife?
20 January – Feeling blue.
23 January – At last!
24 January. – The ecstasy returns.
25 January. – Ecstasy.
26 January. – Still him. His lips. Bliss.
27 January. – The world is an unkind place.
29 January. – Ah! Can't stay here! . . . Must get away! . . .

From time to time Maigret glances up, while Félicie pretends to ignore him.

He tries to be jocular, but his laughter rings as false as that of the traveller who attempts to take liberties with a

hotel chambermaid and keeps the tone light with sugges-
tive banter.

'What's his name?'

'None of your business.'

'Married, is he?'

An angry glare, like a cat defending her kittens.

'Was it love? The real thing?'

She does not reply, but he persists and hates himself for
persisting. He keeps telling himself he's wrong, he thinks of
Rue Lepic, Rue Fontaine, of the scared young man who has
been going backwards and forwards since last night and
keeps crashing into walls like a panic-stricken bumble-bee.

'So tell me, was it here that you met this man?'

'Why not?'

'Did your employer know?'

No. He can't go on like this, interrogating this girl who
does not give a damn about him or his questions. Still, going
round to see Madame Chochoi, as he does next, is not much
more clever. He leans his bike against the shop front and
waits until a woman who is buying a tin of peas has gone.

'Incidentally, Madame Chochoi, did Monsieur Lapie's
housekeeper have many boyfriends?'

'I expect she had some.'

'What do you mean?'

'At least she used to talk about one. Always the same
one. But that's her business. She was often down in the
dumps, poor thing.'

'A married man?'

'Could have been. That was probably why she was
always talking about setbacks. She never said much to

46

me. If she ever told anyone about it, it would have been Léontine, the girl who cleans for Monsieur Forrentin.'

A man has been murdered and here's Maigret, a serious man, a man in the prime of life, worrying his head about the love-life of a girl with a head full of romantic notions! Romantic to the point where there are whole pages in her diary like:

17 June – Feeling down.
18 June – Feeling blue.
21 June – The world is a false paradise in which there isn't enough happiness to go round.
22 June – I love him.
23 June – I love him.

Maigret moves on to Forrentin's house and rings the bell. Léontine, the estate manager's housemaid, is a girl of about twenty, with a large moon face. She immediately takes fright. She is afraid of getting her friend into trouble.

'Of course she used to tell me everything. Or at least everything she wanted to tell me. She used to come round often, rush in she would . . .'

He pictures the two of them so clearly, one open-mouthed in admiration, and Félicie with her coat worn carelessly over her shoulders.

'Anyone else here? Oh Léontine, if you only knew . . .'

She talks and talks the way young women talk among themselves.

'I saw him . . . Oh, I'm so happy!'

Poor Léontine does not know how to answer Maigret's questions.

'I'll never say a bad word about her. Félicie has been so unhappy!'

'On account of a man?'

'Several times she said she wished she was dead.'

'Didn't he love her?'

'I don't know. Stop tormenting me.'

'Do you know his name?'

'She never told me.'

'Did you ever see him?'

'No.'

'Where did she used to meet him?'

'I dunno.'

'Was she his mistress?'

Léontine blushes and stammers:

'Once, she told me that if she ever had a baby . . .'

What has any of this to do with the murder of the old man? But Maigret ploughs on and the further he goes the more he feels plagued by that uneasy feeling he has whenever he is about to make a blunder.

It can't be helped! Here he is, back again on the terrace of the Anneau d'Or. The woman who operates the post office switchboard is waving.

'There have already been two calls from Paris. They'll be calling you back any minute now . . .'

Janvier again? No, it's not his voice, it is a voice unfamiliar to the inspector.

'Hello? Monsieur Maigret?'

So it's not anybody from Quai des Orfèvres.

'I'm a waiter in the buffet at Saint-Lazare station . . . A customer asked me to phone you and say . . . Wait a moment . . . I've gone and forgotten his name . . . A name like one of the months . . . Février? . . .'

'Janvier.'

'That's it! . . . He got on the Rouen train. He couldn't hang about . . . He thinks you could maybe get to Rouen to meet the train . . . He said if you get a car . . .'

'Anything else?'

'No, monsieur . . . I've done what he asked . . . That's the lot . . .'

What does this mean? If Janvier has suddenly got on a train to Rouen, then it can only be because Pétillon is on his way there. He hesitates for a moment. Stepping out of the phone booth, which is stiflingly hot, he wipes his face under the inquisitive gaze of the woman on the switchboard. A car, he should be able to find a car . . .

'But the hell with it!' he growls. 'Just let Janvier handle it himself.'

His search of the three rooms has yielded nothing except Félicie's diary. Lucas is still bored with kicking his heels outside Cape Horn, and the people in the houses close by peep out at him through their curtains from time to time.

So instead of launching himself on the trail of the strange nephew, Maigret has a snack on the terrace of the inn, savours his coffee, tops it off with a glass of old marc and, heaving a sigh, gets back on his bike. As he passes, he hands Lucas a packet of sandwiches and rides down the slope into Poissy.

It doesn't take him long to track down the bar where

Félicie goes dancing on Sundays. It is a wooden structure on the Seine. At this time of day, there's no one there. It's the owner himself, a muscle man wearing a sweater, who asks what he wants. The two men recognize each other, and five minutes later they are sitting at a table in front of a couple of liqueur glasses. It's a small world. The man, who spends Sundays collecting the money before each dance starts, used to be a small-time fairground wrestler who has had a few run-ins with the police. He was first to recognize the inspector.

'I'm guessing you're not here on my account? I'm straight these days and doing well, you know!'

'Of course . . . Of course,' says Maigret with a smile.

'As for the customers . . . No, inspector, I don't think there's anything here for you . . . Errand girls, kitchen-maids, a crowd of harmless kids who . . .'

'Do you know Félicie?'

'Who?'

'A strange girl thin as a rake, with a pointed nose, a stubborn look on her face, always dressed like a flag or a rainbow . . .'

'The Parakeet!'

Well, well! Old Lapie used to call Félicie a cockatoo.

'What's she done?'

'Nothing. I'd just like to know who she used to meet when she came here.'

'Nobody, or near enough . . . My wife – don't beat your brains, you don't know her, she's the genuine article – my wife, as I was saying, called her the Princess on account of the airs she gave herself. What exactly was eating the

50

chick? I never knew. She really did show up like she actually was a princess. When she danced she was as stiff as a board. If you asked her anything, she sort of gave the impression that she wasn't what people thought she was, that she came here incognito. All nonsense, of course! Oh, and she always sat at this table, by herself. She'd sip her drink with her little finger sticking out. Her ladyship didn't dance with just anybody . . . Sunday . . . Ah! that reminds me . . .'

Maigret pictures the crowd on the dance-floor which shakes, the racket of the accordion, the owner standing hands on hips waiting to pass among the couples to collect the dance money.

'She was dancing with a guy I've seen around some place. But where, I'm damned if I can recollect. Short, muscular, nose a bit crooked . . . Anyway. All I know is that he was holding her pretty close . . . Then all at once, in the middle of a dance, she slaps his face with the flat of her hand! I thought there was going to be trouble. I went up to them. But no bother. The guy just left, he'd had enough, and the Princess went snootily back to her seat and started powdering her nose . . .'

Janvier must have got to Rouen ages ago. Maigret leaves his bike on the terrace of the Anneau d'Or, then goes for a word with the woman working the switchboard in the cool interior of the post office.

'No calls for me?'

'Just a message. You're to contact the Rouen central police station. Want me to put you through?'

It's not Janvier he gets at the other end of the line, but the station head.

'Detective Chief Inspector Maigret? . . . This is what we've been asked to pass on to you. The young man got to Rouen after traipsing round a dozen bars in Montmartre. Apparently, he did not speak to anyone. Each time, he seemed to be waiting for somebody. When he got to Rouen, he headed straight for the garrison district. He went into a brasserie I'm sure you know of, the Tivoli, where working girls hang out. He stayed for maybe half an hour, then he wandered through the streets and turned up back at the station. He was looking more tired than ever, even desperate. At present, he's waiting for the Paris train, and Inspector Janvier is staying on his tail . . .'

Maigret gives the standard orders: question the madam who runs the bar, find out which woman Pétillon came to see, what he was after, etc. He is still in the booth when he hears a muffled rumble, like a passing bus, but when he comes out into the post office he realizes that it is the distant herald of an approaching storm.

'Will you be expecting any more calls?' asks the telephone operator, who has never known such thrills in all her days.

'Possibly. I'll send you my sergeant.'

'It's ever so exciting being in the police! Whereas we in our small corner never see anything!'

He gives a mechanical smile instead of shrugging his shoulders as he would like to do and then he sets off once more along the short stretch of road which separates him from the village.

'She's got to start talking!' he keeps telling himself all the way there.

The storm is building. The horizon has turned a threatening purple, and the slanting rays of the sun seem more sharply angled. The flies are biting.

'Go back to the Anneau d'Or, Lucas. Answer the phone calls, if there are any.'

When he opens the door of Cape Horn, his face wears the determined expression of a man who has allowed himself to be walked over for too long. That's all over now! He's going to face up to Félicie, confound her! He'll shake her as hard as it takes to knock her off her high horse!

'That's it, girl! We've finished playing games!'

He knows she's in. He saw a curtain twitch on the ground floor when he was sending Lucas back to Orgeval. He goes in. Silence. In the kitchen, the coffee is percolating. No one in the garden, He scowls.

'Félicie!' he calls softly. 'Félicie!'

He starts to lose patience and he shouts angrily:

'Félicie!'

For a moment he wonders if she hasn't taken him for a ride once again, and whether she hasn't just slipped through his fingers. But no. He hears a faint sound upstairs, something resembling the sobbing of a very small child. He climbs the stairs two at a time and comes to a stop at the door to Félicie's bedroom and then sees her lying full length on her divan.

She is crying, her face buried in the pillow. Just as large tears start to flow, a draught slams a door shut somewhere in the house.

53

'Well?' he growls.

She does not move. Her back jerks with each sob. He puts a hand on her shoulder.

'Well, Félicie?'

'Leave me alone . . . Please, let me be!'

A thought enters his head, but he does not linger over it: this is all just play-acting. Félicie has picked her moment. She has even chosen her posture carefully, and who knows if it's by accident that her dress has ridden up well above her restless knees?

'Come on, up you get.'

Surprise! She does what she's told! Félicie does what she's told without arguing, which is unexpected to say the least. Now she is sitting on her bed, eyes swimming with tears and face mottled with red, and she stares at him, cutting such a dismal, weary figure that he feels as if he is behaving like a brute.

'What's the matter? Come on, tell me . . .'

She shakes her head. She can't speak. She intimates that she would like to tell him everything, but that she can't, and again she buries her head in her hands.

Standing in that room, he feels he looms too large and pulls a chair towards him, sits by the side of the bed and hesitates about whether he should take one of her hands and ease it away from her tear-stained face. For he is not yet convinced by her. He wouldn't be at all surprised if, behind those clenched fists, he were to find a sarcastic expression on her face.

She is crying genuinely. She cries like a child and is not

looking for effect or for sympathy. So it is in a child's voice that at last she stammers:

'You're not being very nice . . .'

'Me, not nice? Oh come on, my girl. Just calm down. Don't you realize that it's for your own good?'

She says no with a shake of her head.

'But damn it all, don't you understand that there's been a murder, that you are the only person who knew the house well enough to . . . I'm not saying you killed the man you lived with here . . .'

'I didn't "live" with him . . .'

'I know. You already told me . . . So let's say he was your father. Because that's what you've been hinting at, isn't it? And let's say that a long time ago old Lapie did something stupid and that later he brought you here, to his house . . . So you stand to inherit everything. You're the one who has gained most from his death.'

He has moved too quickly. She gets to her feet, stands in front of him straight and stiff, the very picture of indignation.

'But it's true, Félicie! . . . Sit down . . . Logically I should have arrested you already.'

'I'm ready . . .'

Good God, it's difficult! How much more would Maigret have preferred to be faced with the wiliest of rogues, the most vicious old reprobates! Deciding when she's play-acting and when she is being serious is impossible. Is she actually ever sincere? He senses that she is observing him, that she never stops watching him with quite frightening lucidity.

'That's not the issue. The issue is that you must start helping us. The man who took advantage of your absence at the grocer's to kill your . . . let's just say, to kill Jules Lapie, was sufficiently familiar with the domestic routine here to . . .'

She sits down wearily on the edge of the bed and murmurs:

'I'm listening.'

'Anyway, why would Lapie take someone he didn't know to his bedroom? He was killed in his room. He had no reason to go upstairs at that time of day. He was busy in the garden. He offered his visitor a drink, though he was pretty *near* . . .'

At times Maigret has almost to shout to make himself heard above the noise of the storm, and when one clap of thunder comes, louder than the rest, Félicie instinctively reaches out her hand and grabs his wrist.

'I'm scared.'

She is shaking. No pretence. She really is shaking.

'There's no need to be frightened. I'm here . . .'

It's a stupid thing to say, and he knows it. She immediately takes advantage of his temporary distraction to put on a more pained face and she moans:

'Why are you tormenting me like this? The way you're going on, you'll only make it even more hurtful! I'm so unhappy! Oh God! How unhappy I am! And you . . . you . . .'

She stares at him with eyes that are wide open, beseeching.

'You're picking on me because I'm weak, because I've got nobody to defend me . . . There's been a man outside the house all last night and all today and he'll be there again tonight . . .'

'What's the name of the man whose face you slapped when you were out dancing last Sunday?'

For a moment she is wrong-footed but then with an unpleasant laugh she says:

'You see!'

'What do I see?'

'I'm the one you're after. It's me you're picking on as if . . . as if you hated me! What did I do to you? I'm begging you! Tell me, what did I ever do to you?'

This would be the moment for Maigret to stand up, put an end to this charade and start talking seriously. That is exactly what he intends to do. The very last thing he wants at this moment would be someone outside, on the landing, watching what he was doing. But it's too late! He has been too slow getting into the driving seat, and Félicie, becoming more intense, uses a roll of thunder as a pretext for clinging on to him, talking into his ear: he feels her warm breath on his cheek and sees her face almost touching his.

'Is it because I am a woman? Are you like Forrentin?'

'What has Forrentin . . . ?'

'He wants me. He follows me around. He told me he would have me sooner or later, that in the end I'd . . .'

It could be true. Maigret remembers the estate manager's face, his rather disconcerting smile and those large, sensual hands . . .

'If that's what you want, say so! I'd much prefer . . .'

'No, girl, no.'

57

This time, he gets up and pushes her off him.

'Come downstairs, please. There is nothing for us in this room.'

'You're the one who came up here.'

'That's no reason for staying here and especially not so that you can put such ideas in my head. Come downstairs. Please . . .'

'Give me a moment to make myself presentable.'

She powders her nose quickly in the mirror. She sniffles.

'You're going to make something awful happen, see if you don't!'

'Like what?'

'I don't know. But if I'm found dead . . .'

'Don't be silly. Come . . .'

He stands back and lets her go first. The storm has so darkened the sky that he has to switch on the light in the kitchen. The coffee on the stove is boiling away.

'I think that I'd like to get away from here,' says Félicie as she turns off the gas.

'Where would you go?'

'Anywhere. I've no idea. Yes. I'll go away, and no one will ever find me. I was wrong to come back.'

'You won't leave.'

Through gritted teeth she murmurs too quietly for him to know if he had heard her correctly:

'We'll see!'

On the off-chance he says:

'If you're thinking of catching up with young Pétillon, I can tell you now that at this moment he's in a brasserie full of women in Rouen.'

'That's not . . .' She corrects herself quickly: 'What's that got to do with me?'

'Is it him?'

'What? What are you getting at?'

'Is he your lover?'

She laughs derisively.

'A boy who's not twenty?'

'Be that as it may, Félicie, but if he's really the one you're trying to shield . . .'

'I'm not trying to shield anyone . . . That's enough! I'm not answering any more questions. You've no right to be hanging round here all day, pestering me. I'll complain.'

'Be my guest!'

'You think you're so clever, don't you. And you've got the upper hand! So you pick on a poor girl because you know she can't defend herself.'

He puts his hat on his head and, despite the rain, reaches the front door, intending to go back to the Anneau d'Or. He doesn't even say goodbye. He's had enough. He's got it wrong. He's going to have to go back to square one and restart the inquiry on another tack.

Too bad if he gets soaked to the skin! As he takes a step forwards, Félicie comes running.

'Don't go!'

'Why not?'

'You know why. Don't go. I'm afraid of the storm . . .'

It's quite true. For once, she is not lying. She is shaking all over, she begs him to stay, she is really grateful when he goes back into the kitchen, sits down – in a bad mood, certainly – but down he sits nevertheless, and by way of thanks she wastes no time in asking:

'Would you like a cup of coffee? Do you want me to pour you a little glass of something?'

She tries to smile and, as she puts the glass down in front of him, she repeats:

'Why are you being so hard on me? What have I ever done to you?'

4. *The Shot from the Taxi*

Maigret is walking along Rue Pigalle at a leisurely pace, with his hands in the pockets of his overcoat, because it's after midnight, and the storm has brought down the temperature. There are still patches of damp on the pavements. Beneath the illuminated signs, nightclub doormen soon spot him as he passes. Customers standing around the horseshoe counter in the bar-cum-tobacconist's on the corner of Rue Notre-Dame-de-Lorette eye each other questioningly. An outsider would notice nothing. But from one end to the other of Montmartre, which depends for its existence on nocturnal revellers, there is an imperceptible ripple, like the cat's-paw on the surface of a pond which gives notice of the approaching squall.

Maigret is all too aware of it and is content. Here, at least, he does not have to deal with a young woman who sobs and fights him all the way. As he passes, he recognizes various characters and guesses that the word is being passed from mouth to mouth, even in the dance-hall cloakrooms, where the old crones who preside over them, alerted to the danger, quickly hide small packets of cocaine.

The Pelican is just here, on the left, with its blue neon sign and its black bouncer. Someone steps out of the shadow, falls into step with the inspector and says in a quiet voice:

'Am I glad to see you!'

It's Janvier, who explains with a casual air of indifference which some might mistake for cynicism but is not as deep-seated as it sounds:

'No problems, sir. There was just one thing I was afraid of, that he'd sit at a table by himself to eat. He's shattered.'

The two men linger on the kerb as if enjoying the cool-ness after the rain and Maigret refills his pipe.

'Since Rouen, he's been at the end of his tether. While we were waiting for the train in the buffet I kept thinking he was about to rush me for the big showdown. He's just a kid wet behind the ears.'

Maigret misses nothing of what is happening around him. Because he is standing there, on the kerb, how many people who do not have clear consciences have been dis-creetly giving him a wide berth or concealing items of a compromising nature?

'On the train, he more or less passed out. When we got to Saint-Lazare station, he didn't know what to do, though maybe he was also a little drunk, because he's had a lot to drink since yesterday. In the end he went home to Rue Lepic. He probably freshened up and put on his dinner jacket. He toyed with his food in a cheap eating house in Place Blanche and then came to work . . . Are you going in? Do you need me any more?'

'You get yourself off home to bed, Janvier.'

If Maigret should need anyone, he had left a couple of duty officers back at Quai des Orfèvres.

'Let's get on with it!' he sighed.

He walks into the Pelican, gives a shrug when he sees the black doorman who busies around and thinks he must smile from ear to ear. He decides not to leave his overcoat with the crone in the cloakroom. Jazz music reaches him through the velvet curtains which mask the entrance to the hall. A small bar on the left. Two women who yawn, a spoilt rich kid, already drunk, and the owner of the establishment who comes running.

'Evening,' the inspector growls.

The owner of the joint looks worried.

'Say, this isn't about anything serious, is it?'

'No. Nothing like that.'

He brushes the man aside and sits down in a corner not far from the musicians' dais.

'Whisky?'

'A beer.'

'But you know we don't keep beer.'

'Brandy and water, then.'

Around him, it's obvious the place has seen better days. Maigret is hard put to pick out any paying customers. Are there any at all in this narrow room, where dim lights cast a reddish glow which changes to purple when the band plays a tango? Hostesses. Now that they know who the new customer is, they don't bother dancing with each other and one of them catches up with her embroidery.

On the dais, Pétillon looks even thinner and younger in his dinner jacket than he really is. He is pasty-faced under the long, fair hair, his eyelids are red with exhaustion and tension, and, try as he might, he cannot take his eyes off the inspector, who just sits there and waits.

Janvier was right: he's a pushover. There are unmistakeable signs that show that a man is out on his feet, that his wheels have come off, that his head's in a spin, that there's only one thing he wants: to have done with it, to get it all off his chest. The sense of it is so palpable that for a moment it seems likely that Jacques Pétillon will lay down his sax and rush across the room to Maigret.

A man at such a pitch of fear is not a pretty sight. Maigret has seen it before, there have even been times when he himself has carefully gingered up certain interviews with suspects – some lasting twenty-four hours or more – to bring his man, or rather his patient, to this same point of physical and mental collapse.

This time, it's been none of his doing. He never thought there was anything in the Pétillon angle. He has no sense that it would lead anywhere. He paid it little attention, being mesmerized by the strange phenomenon that is Félicie, whom he cannot get out of his mind.

He tastes his drink. Pétillon must be astonished to see him behaving so casually. His hands with their long, slim fingers, are shaking. The other members of the band throw him furtive glances.

What had he spent those forty-eight hours of sheer madness looking for so desperately? What hopes had he been clinging to? Whom had he been hoping to find in those cafés and bars where he had gone one after the other, his eyes fervently fixed on the door, finding only disappointment, walking out, searching elsewhere, eventually heading out to Rouen, where he made straight for a bar known for its girls in the garrison part of town?

He is totally drained. Even if Maigret were not there, he would turn himself in of his own accord; he would be seen stumbling up the dusty staircase of police head-quarters and asking to talk to someone.

Ah! Here we go! The band takes a short break. The accordionist drifts towards the bar for a drink. The others talk among themselves in whispers. Pétillon hooks his instrument on to its stand then goes down the two steps.

'I must talk to you . . .' he stammers.

The inspector replies in a very gentle voice:

'I know, boy.'

Is this the right place? Maigret runs his eyes over their surroundings, which make him feel nauseous. There's nothing to be gained by making a spectacle of the boy – he'll probably start blubbing at any moment

'Not thirsty?'

Pétillon shakes his head.

'In that case, let's go . . .'

Maigret pays for his drink, although the club's owner rushes forwards to say it's on the house.

'Look . . . I think you're going to have to do without your saxophone-player tonight. We're both going out for a breather . . . Pétillon, get your hat and coat.'

'I haven't got a coat.'

They're hardly outside on the pavement before he takes a deep breath and dives in:

'Listen, inspector . . . It's best if I tell you everything . . . I can't go on like this . . .'

He is all of a tremble. He must be seeing the lights in

the street dancing all round him. The owner of the Pelican and the black doorman watch them go.

'In your own time, boy . . .'

He'll take him back to headquarters; it's the simplest way. How many investigations have ended in Maigret's office at this time of night, when the entire Police Judiciaire building is deserted, a single officer stands guard at the main entrance and the lamp with the green shade casts a strange light on the man who has cracked.

This one is just a kid. Maigret feels peevish. Really! In this case he has such sub-standard opponents to deal with!

'In here.'

He steers him into a brasserie in Place Pigalle. He needs a beer before he hails a taxi.

'What are you having?'

'I don't care . . . I swear, inspector, I never . . .'

'Of course you didn't. You can tell me all about it soon enough . . . Two beers, waiter!'

He gives a shrug. Two more customers who recognize him and prefer to abandon their onion soup and clear out. Another goes into the call-box, where, through the diamond-shaped window, he can be seen hunched over the public phone.

'Are you sleeping with her?'

'Who?'

Aha! The kid is genuinely amazed: there are inflections in his voice which are unmistakeable.

'Félicie.'

And Pétillon repeats, like someone who has never ever thought of such a thing and does not understand:

'Me? Sleep with Félicie?'

He's all at sea. He was about to launch into a dramatic confession, and now this man who holds his fate in his hands, this Maigret who unleashed a whole pack of plain-clothes officers on his trail, is talking about his uncle's housekeeper!

'I swear, inspector . . .'

'Good . . . Come on, let's go . . .'

They are being overheard. Two small women, pretending to powder their noses. There's nothing to be gained by providing the floor show.

They are now outside again. A few metres away, in the darkness of Place Pigalle, a line of cabs is waiting, and Maigret is about to hail one; he already has his arm up. Not far away, on a corner of the street, a uniformed police-man is looking vaguely around him.

At that exact moment, a shot rings out. The inspector has the impression that there is a second shot almost at the same instant as the first, and a taxi revs and drives off towards Boulevard Rochechouart.

It all happens so quickly that it takes him a second or two to notice that the man at his side is clutching his chest, though he stays on his feet, swaying, reaching out with his other hand for something to hang on to. Mechanically he asks:

'Are you hit?'

The policeman is running towards the line of cabs. He gets into the driving seat of one of them, and it roars into life. A public-spirited driver jumps on to the running board.

Pétillon falls to the ground, his hand pressed to the front

of his dress shirt. He tries to call out, but the only sound he makes is a peculiar and ridiculously feeble croak.

The next morning, the papers publish only a brief paragraph:

Late last night, in Place Pigalle, a jazz musician named as Jacques P . . . was hit in the chest by a bullet fired by an unknown assailant, who got away in a taxi. A manhunt was set up immediately but all efforts to apprehend the armed aggressor proved fruitless.

It is thought that the affair involved a settling of accounts or a crime of passion.

The victim, who is in a critical condition, was taken to Beaujon Hospital. The police are pursuing their inquiries.

This is incorrect. The police do not always issue factually accurate statements to the press. But it is true that Jacques Pétillon is in Beaujon Hospital. It is also true that his condition is serious, so serious that it is not sure that he will live. His left lung was punctured by a large-calibre bullet.

The manhunt is another invention. When he arrives in the office of the commissioner of the Police Judiciaire to give his morning report, Maigret speaks bitterly:

'It was all my fault, sir. I felt like a beer. I also wanted the kid to pull himself together a bit before coming here with me. He was ready to snap. He'd been led a merry dance all day. But I was wrong, obviously . . .

'But I'll say one thing: whoever it was who took advantage of this situation wasn't born yesterday . . .

'When I heard the shot, my first thought was to look after the boy. I let the uniformed officer lead the pursuit. You've read his report? The taxi led him at high speed to the other end of Paris, to Place d'Italie, where it pulled up suddenly. There was no passenger inside.

'We've arrested the taxi-driver, despite his protests. All the same, I've been well and truly had . . .'

He runs a furious eye over the statement made by the taxi-driver after he was interviewed:

I was parked up in Place Pigalle when a man I never saw before offered me 200 francs to play a trick on one of his friends, his very words . . . He was going to let off a cracker – that's the actual word he used – and, when I heard it go bang, all I was to do was take off as fast as I could and drive all the way to Place d'Italie . . .

Which sounds rather too unvarnished coming from a cabbie who works nights! But it will be difficult to prove that he's lying.

I didn't get much of a look at the man, who was standing in shadow by the bushes round the fountain, holding his head down. He was broad in the shoulder and wore a dark suit and a grey hat.

A description which could apply to any number of men!

'This is one shambles that I won't forget in a hurry, I can assure you,' growls Maigret. 'Whoever thought up a stunt like that is . . . He crouches between two taxis or in a patch

69

of shadow. He fires. At the same moment the taxi drives off, and naturally everybody assumes the assassin is in it, and someone sets off in pursuit, while our man has had all the time in the world to make his escape or even to blend in with the crowd . . . The other taxi-drivers who were parked there have been questioned. None of them saw anything. One, an old hand I've known for years, thinks he saw a figure walking round the fountain.'

Imagine! The saxophone player was ready to talk, in a mood to tell everything even when he was still in the Pelican, and Maigret was responsible for not letting him speak! Now, God only knows when he'll be fit for questioning, if, that is, he ever will be.

'What are you planning to do now?'

There is the classic approach. The attempted murder took place in Montmartre, within a defined perimeter. Fifty or so people to interview, all already known to the police, who just happened to be in the area, in fact all those who reacted liked crabs in a basket when news of the presence of Detective Chief Inspector Maigret went the rounds of Rue Pigalle.

Of that number a few are not snow-white lambs. By pushing them, by threatening them and looking more closely into their petty dealings, it is possible to extract information from them.

'I'll get a couple of men on it, sir. Meanwhile, I . . .'

There is nothing for it: he is irresistibly drawn elsewhere. As he has been from the start, from the very first day he set foot in that cardboard cut-out world of Jeanneville.

Shouldn't his reluctance to put a distance between

himself and Cape Horn and the erratic Félicie have been a kind of warning?

Events had proved him wrong. All the indications now are that it is around Place Pigalle that the search for the truth about the death of old Lapie should be centred.

'Even so, I'm going back out to the sticks . . .'

Pétillon had just had enough time to tell him one thing: he wasn't sleeping with Félicie. He looked totally bewildered when Maigret talked about her, as if it had never even crossed his mind to think . . .

It is now 8.30 a.m. Maigret phones his wife.

'That you? . . . No, nothing special . . . I don't know when I'll be home . . .'

She's used to it. He stuffs the reports into his pockets. Among them is one from Rouen giving the pedigree of all the girls who work at the Tivoli. Pétillon did not *go upstairs* with any of them. When he went in, he hid himself away in a corner. Two of the girls sat down next to him on the crimson plush wall seat.

'Isn't there a girl here called Adèle?' he'd asked.

'You're behind the times, kid. Adèle hasn't been around here for ages. You mean a small, dark-haired girl with boobs like pears, is that her?'

He doesn't know. All he knows is that he's looking for a girl called Adèle, who was working in this brasserie the previous year. She's been gone for months. No one knows where she is. If he was going to have to go looking for all the Adèles in all the brothels in France . . .

One inspector has been despatched to make a thorough search of the saxophone player's room in Rue Lepic.

Janvier, who hasn't had much of a chance to rest for long, will spend the day in and around Place Pigalle.

While that is happening, Maigret has taken the train at Saint-Lazare station, gets out at Poissy and starts walking up the slope to Jeanneville.

It seems that after the previous day's storm the fields have become even greener, the sky a more delicate blue. Soon he comes in sight of the pink houses. He waves at Madame Chochoi, who stares back blankly through her window as he passes by.

He goes straight to find Félicie. Why does he feel so pleased by the prospect? Why does he unconsciously quicken his step? He smiles at the thought of seeing Lucas's glum face after an overnight stake-out of Cape Horn. He sees him from a distance, sitting by the side of the road, an unlit pipe between his teeth. He must be feeling sleepy. He must be feeling hungry.

'Had a hard time, Lucas? Anything happened?'

'Nothing, sir. But I could fancy a cup of coffee and bed. The coffee first . . .'

His eyes are puffy with lack of sleep, his overcoat is worn, his shoes and the bottoms of his trousers are covered with reddish mud.

'Take yourself off to the Anneau d'Or. There's been a development.'

'What?'

'The musician's taken a hit . . .'

It might seem that the inspector is callous, but Sergeant Lucas is not taken in, and moments later he is walking away, shaking his head.

Best foot forwards! Maigret looks all round him with the satisfaction of one who finds himself back in familiar surroundings, then strides towards the front door of the house. But no. He decides instead to walk round the building and go in through the garden. He pushes the side-gate . . . The kitchen door is open.

He stands rooted for a moment, stunned by surprise, and then wonders whether he's not about to start laughing. Hearing his footsteps, Félicie has come to the door, where she stands very straight, confronting him with a stern expression on her face.

What on earth is the matter with her now? What is it that makes her look so different? It's not because she has been crying that her eyes look so puffy and her face covered with red blotches.

As he walks towards her, she says in a voice which is more acid than ever:

'Well? Are you satisfied now?'

'What's happened? Did you fall down the stairs?'

'What's the point of standing a policeman outside the house night and day! I assume your guard-dog was asleep on the job?'

'Slow down, Félicie, say it more clearly . . . You're not trying to make me believe . . .'

'That the murderer came and that he attacked me? Yes, I am! Isn't that what you wanted?'

Maigret was intending to talk to her about Pétillon and last night's shooting, but decides that first he'd rather hear more about what has been going on at Cape Horn.

'Come and sit yourself down. Here, in the garden, that's

it! Don't look so sorry for yourself! . . . Now, stay calm, don't look so fierce, just tell me nicely what happened. When I left you yesterday evening, you were overwrought. What have you been up to?'

'Nothing,' she said disdainfully.

'Very well, I assume that first you ate . . . then you locked up and went upstairs to your room . . . All right so far? Are you quite sure you locked the doors?'

'I always lock the door before I go to bed.'

'So you got into bed . . . What time was it?'

'I waited downstairs until the storm had passed.'

It was of course true that he had been callous enough to leave her alone despite her fear of thunder and lightning!

'Did you drink anything?'

'Just coffee . . .'

'To help you to sleep, no doubt . . . What next?'

'I read.'

'For a long time?'

'I don't know. Maybe until midnight. I turned the light off. I was sure something terrible was going to happen . . . I did warn you.'

'Now tell me what that something terrible was.'

'You're making fun of me . . . But I don't care . . . You think you're so clever, don't you! . . . Well, at some point, I heard a sort of scraping noise coming from Monsieur Lapie's room . . .'

Of course. Maigret does not believe a word of what she is telling him and as he listens and observes her, he wonders what she's up to with this new fabrication. Lying comes to her as naturally as breathing. The local police chief at Fécamp had phoned with some information as requested.

Maigret knows now that Félicie's insinuations about the nature of her connection with Jules Lapie were pure invention. Actually she has a father and mother. Her mother takes in washing, and her father is an old drunk who roams around the docks, lending a hand here, helping out there, especially when it means being stood small shots of strong, rotgut brandy. Questioning local men and the most gossipy of the neighbours yielded nothing: old Lapie had never had any close relations with the laundress. When he needed someone to keep house for him, his brother, the ship's carpenter, pointed him in the direction of Félicie, who used to come sometimes to his place to help with the housework.

'Right, so you heard a sort of scraping sound . . . Naturally you threw open the window immediately to call the policeman who was standing guard outside.'

He has spoken with heavy irony, but she shakes her head.

'Why not?'

'Because!'

'Because, I can only suppose, you didn't want the man you assumed to be in the room across the landing to be arrested?'

'Perhaps!'

'Go on . . .'

'I got out of bed, without making a noise . . .'

'And without putting the light on either, I expect. Because if you'd switched it on, Sergeant Lucas would

75

have seen it. The shutters don't close properly . . . So, you're out of bed . . . You're not afraid, though an ordinary storm scares you to death . . . What happened then? Did you leave your bedroom?'

'Not straight away. I put my ear against the door and listened. There was someone on the other side of the landing. I heard a chair being moved. Then what sounded like a stifled curse. I knew then that the man couldn't find what he was looking for and that he was getting ready to leave . . .'

'Was your bedroom door locked?'

'Yes.'

'But you opened it so you could rush out, unarmed, and confront a man who was probably the murderer of Jules Lapie?'

'Yes.'

She glares in defiance. He gives a little whistle of admiration.

'So you were quite sure he wouldn't harm you? Obviously you had no way of knowing that at exactly that time young Pétillon was far from here, in Paris . . .'

She cannot help exclaiming:

'What do you know about that?'

'Let's see . . . What time was it?'

'I looked at the time *after*. It was half past three in the morning. How do you know that Jacques . . .'

'Ah! You call him by his Christian name?'

'Oh, why don't you just leave me alone! If you don't believe me, why don't you just go!'

'Fair enough, I won't interrupt again . . . So, you

came out of your room, full of spirit, armed only with courage . . .'

'And got punched in the face!'

'The man ran away?'

'Went out through the door into the garden. That's the way he came in.'

Actually, Maigret would love to tell her, despite the bruises to her face:

'Know something? I don't believe a word of it.'

On the other hand, if it could be shown that she'd caused her injuries herself, would it have made a difference? Why?

But at this juncture, his eye is caught by something, and he stares intently at the still-damp earth of a flower bed. She notices and, looking in the same direction, sees the footprints and through a thin smile says:

'Perhaps it was my feet that made those marks?'

He stands up.

'Come . . .'

He goes into the house. He has no difficulty seeing the muddy trail on the polished treads of the staircase. He opens the door of the old man's bedroom.

'You came in here?'

'Yes. But I didn't touch anything.'

'What about this chair? Was it just here last night?'

'No. It was by the window.'

At present, it is in front of the huge walnut wardrobe, and on its woven straw seat distinct traces of mud are visible.

So Félicie wasn't lying after all. A man really did break into Cape Horn during the night, and it could not have been Pétillon, who, at that moment, poor devil, was lying on an operating table in Beaujon Hospital.

If Maigret needed further proof, he finds it when he in turn stands on the chair and looks on the top of the wardrobe, where fingers have disturbed the thick layer of dust and where someone has used a tool to prise up a strip of wood.

He'll have to call in experts from Criminal Records to photograph everything and take fingerprints, if there are any.

More serious now, with a worried expression on his face, Maigret mutters, seemingly to himself:

'And you didn't call for help! You knew there was a police officer outside the window and you did nothing. You even took great care not to switch any lights on.'

'I switched the light on in the kitchen when I was bathing my face in cold water.'

'But wasn't that because the kitchen light can't be seen from the road? In other words, you did not want to raise the alarm. Despite being punched, you wanted to give your attacker time to get away. This morning, you got up as if nothing had happened and you still didn't call the sergeant.'

'I knew you'd come.'

Oddly enough – it's childish and he hates himself for it – he feels somewhat flattered that she waited for him to come instead of turning to Lucas. He is even secretly grateful for that 'I knew you'd come'!

He leaves the room, locking the door behind him. It is also clear that this unusual burglar didn't look anywhere other than on the top of the wardrobe. He did not open drawers or search in dark corners. So he must have known . . .

In the kitchen, Félicie glances at her reflection in the mirror.

'You said just now that you were with Jacques last night . . .'

He takes a good, long look at her. She is shaken, of that there is no question. She waits, visibly distressed. Then, in a lighter tone, he says:

'You told me yesterday that he wasn't your lover, that he was just a boy . . .'

She does not respond.

'He had an accident last night. Someone took a shot at him in the middle of a street . . .'

She exclaims:

'Is he dead? Tell me! Is Jacques dead?'

He is tempted. Does she ever think twice about lying? Aren't the police entitled to use any means available to track down criminals? He is sorely tempted to say yes. Who knows how she would react? Who knows if . . .

But he can't bring himself to do it. He sees her there, far too distressed, and instead he looks away and mutters:

'No, you can set your mind at rest. He's not dead. Just wounded.'

She sobs. Holding her head in both hands, wild-eyed, she cries desperately:

'Jacques! Jacques! My own Jacques!'

Then an explosion of fury. She turns to the placid man who avoids her eye:

'And you were there, weren't you? And you let it happen! I hate you, do you hear, I hate you! It's your fault, it's all your fault that . . .'

She collapses on to a chair and continues crying, bent double, with her head on the kitchen table next to the coffee-grinder.

From time to time the same words are repeated:

' . . . Jacques! . . . My own Jacques! . . .'

Is it because he has a hard heart that Maigret, standing in the doorway, not knowing where to look, steps out into the deserted garden, hesitates, stares at his shadow on the ground and eventually opens the door to the wine store, goes in and draws himself a glass of rosé?

5. *Customer 13*

That morning, Maigret was possessed of a rich fund of patience. But there were limits . . . He had not been able to prevent Félicie putting on her full mourning outfit, with that absurd pancake hat and the crepe veil which she wore as though it were some ancient drapery. And what had she plastered over her face? Was it to hide the bruises? It made you wonder, given that she had such a distinct sense of the occasion. Whatever the reason, she was whey-faced, as palely made up as a clown with cold cream and flour. In the train taking them to Paris, she sat completely still, priestess-like, her eyes painfully distant, giving out the impression that she wanted all around her to think:

'Poor thing! How she must be suffering! And what self-control! She is the very image of grief, the living embodiment of the *mater dolorosa*.'

Not once does Maigret smile. When, in Rue Saint-Honoré, she was about to go into a shop selling early-season fruit and vegetables, he muttered quietly in her ear:

'Félicie, I don't think he's in a fit state to eat anything!'

Didn't he understand? Of course he understood, and when she persisted he let her get on with it. She wanted to buy the finest Spanish grapes, oranges, a bottle of champagne. She insisted on loading herself up with flowers, an immense bouquet of white lilacs, and she carried it all herself, without losing a shred of her tragic, aloof manner.

Maigret resigned himself and followed her like a kindly, indulgent father. He was relieved to learn that it was not visiting time at Beaujon Hospital because, looking the way she did, she would have caused a sensation. He did, however, persuade the duty doctor to allow her to look into the room where Jacques Pétillon was isolated. It was at the end of a long corridor with painted walls, full of stale smells, with open doors through which they saw beds, cheerless faces and whiteness, far too much whiteness which in those surroundings became the colour of sickness.

They were made to wait for some time. Félicie remained standing with her cargo throughout. A nurse came eventually, and he gave a start.

'Give me all that. It will come in useful for some child . . . Sh! Mind, no talking. Don't make a noise . . .'

She opened the door no more than a crack, allowed Félicie only a quick glance into the cubicle shrouded in semi-darkness, where Pétillon lay stretched out like a corpse.

When the door closed, Félicie felt obliged to say:

'You will save him, won't you? Please, please. Do everything you can to save him . . .'

'But mademoiselle . . .'

'Don't think of the expense . . . Here . . .'

Maigret did not laugh, he did not even smile when he saw her open her bag and take out a thousand-franc note folded up small and give it to the nurse.

'If it's a matter of money, no matter how much . . .'

From that point on, Maigret stopped making fun of her, and yet she had never been as ridiculous. There was more. As they walked back along the corridor with Félicie's black veil billowing opulently, a child stepped into her path. She leaned down, intending to hug the sick toddler and sighed:

'Poor darling!'

Are we not more aware of the sufferings of others when we are suffering ourselves? A few feet away stood a young, platinum-haired nurse outrageously squeezed into a uniform which showed every curve. The nurse looked up, almost burst out laughing and called one of her colleagues who was in one of the side wards so that she could see the spectacle too.

'You, mademoiselle, are a birdbrain!' snapped Maigret.

And he continued to escort Félicie as solemnly as if he had been one of the family. She had heard the put-down and was grateful. On the pavement outside, in the sunshine that filled the street, she seemed to be less tense. She found being with him very natural, and he used the moment to murmur:

'You know the whole story, don't you?'

She did not deny it. She looked elsewhere. Her way of admitting it.

'Come on . . .'

It was now a little before noon. Maigret decided to turn right towards the luminous, noisy bustle of Place des Ternes, and she followed, tottering along on heels which were too high.

'But I'm not going to tell you anything,' she breathed after they had gone a few steps.

'I know . . .'

He knew a great deal now. He did not yet know who had killed old Lapie. He did not know the name of the man who shot at the saxophone player the night before, but it would all come to him in its own good time.

Above all, he knew that Félicie . . . How could he put it? In the train, for example, the few passengers who had seen her enfolded in theatrical mourning had thought she was ridiculous; in the hospital, that much too curvaceous nurse had not been able to conceal her amusement; the owner of the dance-hall at Poissy had called her the Parakeet . . . others called her the Princess, Lapie had come up with the label Cockatoo, and for some time now even Maigret's back had been put up by her childish antics . . .

Even now people turned and stared at the odd couple they formed, and when Maigret opened the door of a small neighbourhood restaurant, which was still empty at this time of day, he caught the waiter winking at the proprietress, who was sitting at the till.

The truth is that Maigret had located the simple human heartbeat that lies beneath the most wildly flamboyant exteriors.

'We're going to have a nice lunch together now, all right?'

She felt obliged to repeat:

'But I'm still not going to tell you anything.'

'I've got the message. You won't tell me anything. Now, what do you want to eat?'

The inside of the restaurant is old-fashioned and friendly. The walls are creamy-white, and there are large, patchily clouded mirrors, nickel-plated holders into which the waiter tucks the cloth he uses for wiping his tables, a varnished and grained rack of pigeon-holes, where the regulars keep their serviettes. The dish of the day is written on a board: mutton stew with spring vegetables. On the menu extra charges are marked next to nearly all the dishes.

Maigret has ordered. Félicie has arranged her veil so that it falls behind her, and the weight of it pulls her hair back.

'Were you very unhappy at Fécamp?'

He knows what he is doing. He waits for the quiver of her lips, the defiant expression she is able instinctively to put on her face.

'Why should I have been unhappy?'

True. Why? He knows Fécamp, the small, pinched-looking houses crouching in a line under the east cliffs, the narrow alleyways running with sewage, the children playing in a stomach-turning stench of fish . . .

'How many brothers and sisters do you have?'

'Seven.'

The father a drunk. A mother who washes clothes all day long. He pictures her, a little girl who is too tall, legs like matchsticks, no shoes. She is put to work as a servant at Arsène's, a small restaurant on the docks, and she sleeps in an attic. She is dismissed for stealing a few sous from the till and she does housework on odd days for Ernest Lapie, the Lapie who is a ship's carpenter . . .

She is now eating daintily, almost to the point of holding her little finger in the air, and Maigret does not feel like laughing at her.

'I could have married the son of a ship-owner . . .'

'Of course, Félicie. But you didn't fancy him, did you?'

'I don't like men with red hair. Not to mention the fact that his father had designs on me. Men are such pigs . . .'

It's odd. When you see her a certain way, you forget that she's twenty-four, you just see that restless face, like a little girl's, and you wonder how anyone could ever have taken her seriously.

'Tell me, Félicie . . . Did your . . . I mean, was Pegleg jealous?'

He is pleased with himself. He has anticipated that sharp thrust of the chin, the look which is both surprised and uncertain, the flash of anger in those eyes.

'There was never anything between us.'

'Yes, I know. But that doesn't mean he couldn't be jealous, does it? I'd bet that he forbade you to go dancing at Poissy on Sundays, and you were forced to sneak out . . .'

She does not answer him. No doubt, she is wondering how he has managed to find out about the old man's weird jealousy. He would wait for her every Sunday evening, even coming as far as the top of the slope to watch out for her, and made terrible scenes.

'You let him think you had boyfriends . . .'

'What's stopping me have boyfriends?'

'Nothing! But you told him about them! He called you all sorts of names. I wonder if it ever happened that he hit you?'

'I wouldn't have let him lay a finger on me!'

She's lying! Maigret pictures both of them so clearly!

They were as isolated in that new house, in the middle of the new village of Jeanneville, as castaways on a desert island. There is nothing to connect them to anything. They rub each other up the wrong way from morning to night, they watch each other, argue and need each other: the pair of them form a world of their own.

Pegleg only emerges from that world at set times, when he goes off to play cards in the Anneau d'Or. But Félicie seeks out more rollicking forms of escape.

She would have to be locked up and a guard posted under her windows to stop her running off and going down to the dance hall at Poissy, where she puts on airs like a princess in disguise. As soon as she has a free moment, she scoots off to see Léontine and launches into a frenzy of confidences with her.

The explanation is not so hard to find! The office clerks who crowd into the restaurant and begin eating their lunch as they read their newspapers stare bewilderedly at the exotic creature who has invaded their habitat. There isn't a single one of them who doesn't steal a glance at Félicie from time to time, not one who is not ready to smile or wink at the waiter.

Yet she's only a woman. A child-woman. This is what Maigret has understood and this is why, from now on, he talks to her with affectionate gentleness and indulgence.

Around her he reconstructs life as it was lived at Cape Horn. If old Lapie were still alive, Maigret is sure that he would shock him to the core by telling him point-blank: 'You're jealous of your maid.'

Jealous? Him? He wasn't even in love with the girl, he

had never been in love with anyone in his life! But jealous, oh yes, because she was part of his world, a world so narrow that if the smallest part of it went missing . . .

Did he ever sell the surplus vegetables he grew? Did he sell the fruit from his orchard? Did he ever give them away? No! They were his property. Félicie was also his property. He never allowed just anybody into his house! Only he drank the wine in his store.

'What sort of welcome did he give his nephew?'

'He'd meet him in Paris. When his sister died, he almost took him in at Cape Horn, but Jacques decided he didn't want to. He has his pride.'

'And once, when Lapie went to Paris to collect his quarterly pension, he met his nephew, who was in a pitiful state, wasn't he?'

'What do you mean "pitiful"?'

'Pétillon used to work in Les Halles, unloading vegetables.'

'There's no shame in that!'

'Of course not. No shame at all. On the contrary . . . So he brought him back. He gave him his own bedroom because . . .'

She is furious.

'It wasn't how you think . . .'

'But that didn't stop him keeping a very close eye on the pair of you. What did he find out?'

'Nothing.'

'Did you sleep with Pétillon?'

She bends her head over her plate without saying either yes or no.

'The fact remains that life became impossible, and Jacques Pétillon left.'

'He didn't get on with his uncle.'

'That's what I meant.'

Maigret is pleased. He will cherish a special memory of this simple lunch in the quiet, unremarkable setting of a neighbourhood restaurant. A slanting bar of sunlight on the tablecloth and the jug of red wine. The intimacy between him and Félicie has acquired a softer, almost cordial edge. He is fully aware that if he told her as much, she would deny it and revert to her disdainful posturing, but she is as content to be there as he is, happy to break out of her loneliness, which she always fills instinctively with chaotic thoughts.

'It will work out all right, you'll see . . .'

She is almost prepared to believe him. But then her suspicions regain control. She is constantly afraid of falling into God only knows what traps. There are times – unfortunately of short duration – when she seems to be on the verge of turning into a young woman just like any other. It wouldn't take much for her face to relax completely, for her to look straight at Maigret so that her eyes do not express thoughts which she is not thinking. Tears start to well up, and her features are softened by her weariness . . .

She is about to say something, and a fatherly Maigret is only too glad to encourage her . . .

But alas! At that same instant, there is a hint of a reservation that sits behind that obstinate forehead and again takes her over, and it is in her acid voice that she declares:

'If you think for one moment that I can't see what you're up to . . .'

She feels alone, left all alone to carry the full weight of events on her shoulders. She is the centre of the world. And if proof be needed, a detective chief inspector of the Police Judiciaire, a man like Maigret, is now picking on her, just her!

She does not suspect that even then he is pursuing a considerable number of lines of inquiry. Inspectors are working Place Pigalle and the surrounding streets. At Quai des Orfèvres, men are busy questioning a number of individuals who in the early hours were roused out of their beds in furnished rooms in dubious hotels. In many towns, members of the Vice Squad are busy tracking down a girl named Adèle who some time in the past worked for three months in a Rouen brasserie.

And all that, the plodding routine of police work, will inevitably produce results.

But here, in this small restaurant where the regulars greet each other with guarded nods – though they might eat their lunch at the same table, they have never been formally introduced! – the inspector is looking for something very different: to get to the heart of the affair, not to achieve a mechanical reconstruction of events.

'Do you like strawberries?'

There are strawberries on the sideboard, on cotton-wool, in punnets, the first of the season.

'Waiter . . . Give us . . .'

She is greedy, and strawberries are fun. Or more accurately, she has a taste for rare things. It does not matter that Jacques Pétillon is in no state to eat grapes and oranges or drink champagne. It's the gesture that counts, the sight of those opulent purplish globules and the bottle with the gold-covered neck . . . She would eat strawberries even if she didn't like them.

'What's the matter, Félicie?'

'Nothing.'

She has just turned pale, and this time she is not play-acting. She has had a shock. The strawberry she has in her mouth has got stuck, and it looks very much as if she is about to get up and rush outside. She coughs and buries her face in her handkerchief as people do when something has gone down the wrong way.

'What's the . . . ?'

As he turns round, Maigret catches sight of a small man who, though the weather is warm, removes a thick overcoat and scarf, hangs them on a peg and takes a rolled-up serviette from one of the pigeon-holes, the one numbered 13.

He is middle-aged, greying, unremarkable, one of those colourless individuals who are frequently encountered in cities: solitary, fastidious, pernickety, widowers or confirmed bachelors, whose lives are just a maze of small habits. The waiter serves him without asking what he wants, sets a half-started bottle of mineral water down before him. As he opens his newspaper, the man stares at Félicie and frowns, rummages through his memories and begins to think . . .

'Had enough?'

'I'm not hungry any more. Let's go.'

She has already put her serviette down on the table. Her hand is shaking.

'Calm down, girl.'

'Me? I am calm. Why shouldn't I be?'

From where he is sitting, Maigret can observe number 13 in the mirror on the wall in front of him and he is still following the effort to remember on the man's face . . . He's got it . . . No, that's not it . . . Try again! . . . He tries again . . . He is about to . . . Now he's there! . . . His eyes widen . . . He is astonished . . . He looks as if he is thinking: 'Good grief! Now there's a coincidence!'

But he does not get up and come over to say hello to her. He does not give her any indication that they are known to each other. Where did he meet her? What kind of relationship was it? He gives Maigret a thorough looking over from head to foot, calls the waiter and whispers something to him; the waiter looks as if he's saying he doesn't know, that this is the first time the couple . . .

Meanwhile Félicie, sick with panic, suddenly gets to her feet and lurches in the direction of the washroom. Has her gullet become so restricted that she is about to regurgitate the strawberries which she has just eaten so daintily and with such enjoyment?

In her absence, Maigret and the stranger look at each other more openly. Perhaps customer 13 is thinking of coming over to exchange a few words with Félicie's companion?

The door with frosted glass panes which leads to the cloakroom also leads to the kitchen. The waiter comes and goes. He has red hair! Just like the ship-owner's son who wanted to marry Félicie when she lived at Fécamp. How can he not smile? She takes her cue from whatever catches her eye: she sees a red-haired waiter, she is asked if she had been very unhappy, her brain works with the speed of light and lo! the waiter is transformed into the son of a ship-owner who . . .

She is away a long time, too long for Maigret's liking. The waiter has also been gone for some time. Customer 13 is thinking, thinking like a man who is about to reach a decision.

Eventually she emerges. She is almost smiling. As she returns, she pulls the veil back down over her face. She does not sit down again.

'Coming?'

'I ordered coffee. You like coffee, don't you?'

'Not now. It would only make me jumpy.'

He pretends to go along with this, calls the waiter and looks him straight in the face as he settles the bill. The man's cheeks become slightly flushed. It's so obvious! She has given him a message to give to customer 13. Perhaps she scribbled a few words on a scrap of paper with an instruction not to give it to the person it is intended for until after she has left.

As they leave, the inspector's eye falls accidentally on the heavy overcoat on its peg with its pockets wide open.

'We're going back to Jeanneville now, aren't we?'

She takes his arm with a gesture that might well seem spontaneous.

'I'm so tired! It's been a strain.'

She grows impatient when he just stands there, not moving, on the edge of the pavement, like a man who is undecided.

'What are you thinking? Why aren't you coming? There's a train in half an hour.'

She is horribly afraid. Her hand trembles on Maigret's arm, and he is seized with an odd impulse to reassure her. Then he shrugs his shoulders.

'Of course . . . Taxi! . . . Get in! . . . Saint-Lazare station, suburban lines.'

What a weight of anguish he has taken off her shoulders! In the open-topped taxi, where the sun nuzzles them gently, she feels a need to talk and talk.

'You said you'd stay with me. You did say that, didn't you? Aren't you afraid of how it might look? Are you married? . . . How silly of me. You're wearing a ring.'

An anxious moment at the station. He just buys one ticket. Is he just going to see her to her compartment and then stay behind in Paris? But she has forgotten he has a pass, and he settles heavily on the seat and gives her a look tinged with self-reproach.

He will be able to catch up with grey-haired customer 13 whenever he likes, since the man is a regular at the restaurant. The train shudders, and Félicie believes she is out of danger now. At Poissy, they walk past the café-dansant, where the proprietor, standing at the door of the wooden building, recognizes Maigret and gives him a wink.

The inspector cannot pass up an opportunity to tease Félicie.

'Just a minute, I think I'll ask him if Pegleg ever showed up here and watched you dancing . . .'

She pulls him away.

'No need to bother. He did come, several times.'

'You see? He was jealous after all.'

They climb the slope. Now they're outside Mélanie

Chochoi's shop, and Maigret continues playing the same game.

'What if I go in and ask her how many times she saw you roaming round of an evening with Jacques Pétillon?'

'She never saw us!'

This time she is sure of herself.

'So you made sure you kept out of sight?'

Here is the house, which they see just as a large car from Criminal Records drives off, leaving Lucas standing at the door like some upright, law-abiding householder.

'Who was that?'

'Photographers, experts . . .'

'Of course! Fingerprints!'

She is well informed. She has read lots of novels, including detective stories!

'How're things, Lucas?'

'Not much to report, sir. The intruder wore rubber gloves, just as you said. So they just took casts of his shoe-prints. Brand-new pair. Hadn't been worn more than three days.'

Félicie has gone up to her room to change out of her mourning clothes and remove her veil.

'Anything new with you, sir? It's as if . . .'

He knows him so well! At times Maigret has a way of becoming expansive; he beams and seems to suck in life through his pores. He looks around him now at these surroundings which have grown so familiar that with unconscious mimicry he begins to think and act like the locals.

'Fancy a drop of something?'

He goes to the sideboard in the dining room, takes out the part-full decanter, pours out two liqueur glasses and then stands in the doorway. overlooking the garden.

'Here's to you! . . . Ah, Félicie, tell me . . .'

She has come back down, is wearing an apron and starts busying around making sure the men from Criminal Records haven't left her kitchen in a mess.

'Would you be kind enough to make a cup of coffee for my friend Lucas? I must go round to the Anneau d'Or, but I shall leave you in the sergeant's hands. I'll see you this evening.'

He is expecting that suspicious, anxious glare.

'I really am going to the Anneau d'Or.'

And so he is, but not for long. Since there is no taxi at Orgeval, he asks the garage mechanic, Louvet, to drive him to Paris in his van.

'I need to go to Les Ternes. Go along Rue du Faubourg Saint-Honoré.'

There is no one in the restaurant when he marches in, and the waiter must have been taking a nap somewhere in the back, because he emerges yawning, with his hair ruffled.

'Do you know the address of the man to whom you gave a note from the lady who was with me earlier on?'

The fool thinks he is dealing with a jealous husband or an angry father. He denies everything, starts getting flustered. Maigret shows him his warrant card.

'I don't know his name, that's the truth. He works in this area, but I don't think he lives around here, because he only comes in at lunchtime.'

Maigret has no intention of waiting until tomorrow.

'Do you know what he does?'

'Wait a moment. One day I overheard him talking with the boss . . . I'll go and see if he's still in.'

Obviously, the place is dedicated to the patron saint of the siesta. The landlord appears minus his collar and pushes his untidy hair back with one hand.

'Number 13? He's in leathers and furs. He told me all about it one day, though in connection with what I couldn't say. He works for a firm on Avenue de Wagram.'

With the help of a phone book, Maigret soon comes up with Gellet & Mautoison, Leathers and Furs, Import-Export, 17A Avenue de Wagram. He pays them a call. The clack of typewriters in offices which are darkened by green-tinted windows on which the names of the owners, reading from inside, are reversed.

'You'll be wanting Monsieur Charles. One moment.'

He is led through a maze of corridors and stairs which all reek of untreated fleeces, all the way to a small office under the eaves. On the door is a sign which reads: 'Stationery'.

There he is, Monsieur 13, looking greyer than ever in his long grey overall, which he wears for work. He gives a start when he sees Maigret walk into his private sanctuary,

'Can I help you? . . .'

'Police Judiciaire. Nothing to worry about. Just a few simple questions to ask you . . .'

'I don't see . . .'

'But you do see, Monsieur Charles, you see very well. Show me the note the waiter gave you earlier this afternoon.'

'I swear . . .'

'Don't swear, or I'll be forced to arrest you immediately as an accomplice to murder.'

The man blows his nose noisily, and not as a way of playing for time. He has a permanent cold in the head – hence the thick overcoat and muffler.

'You put me in an embarrassing position . . .'

'But much less embarrassing for you than the one you will land yourself in if you refuse to answer my questions truthfully.'

Maigret is using his big voice, he is coming on *tough*, as Madame Maigret would say, who always finds it very amusing, because she knows him better than anyone.

'Look, inspector, I never thought that what I did . . .'

'First, let me see the note.'

The man does not produce it from his pocket but has to climb a ladder to retrieve it from the top of a set of shelves where he had hidden it behind a stack of headed stationery. He does not return with just the note but with a revolver, which he holds carefully, like a man who is terrified of guns.

Please, don't say anything, ever, for whatever reason. Throw you know what in the Seine. *It's a matter of life and death.*

Maigret smiles at these last words, which are pure Félicie. Didn't she say exactly the same thing to Louvet, the garage mechanic from Orgeval?

'When I noticed . . .'

'You mean when you noticed that you had this gun in the pocket of your overcoat?'

'You know? . . .'

'You'd just got on the Métro train. You were crushed up against a young woman in full mourning, and just as she was making for the door you felt something heavy being slipped into your pocket.'

'I didn't realize until afterwards.'

'And you were scared.'

'I've never handled a gun in my life. I didn't even know if it was loaded. I still don't . . .'

To the horror of the stationery clerk, Maigret releases the cartridge clip, from which there is one bullet missing.

'But because you remembered the girl in the mourning weeds . . .'

'At first, I thought I should hand this . . . this object in to the police . . .'

Monsieur 13 is getting rattled.

'You are the susceptible type, Monsieur Charles. Women unnerve you, don't they? I'd bet that you've never had much to do with them.'

A bell rings. The clerk gazes in a panic at a panel fixed to the front of his desk.

'That's my boss. He wants me . . . Can I . . .'

'Yes, go! I know everything I wanted to know.'

'But that young woman . . . Tell me . . . Did she really . . .'

A shadow appears in Maigret's eyes and then is gone.

'All in good time, Monsieur Charles. Now hurry up. Your boss is getting impatient.'

For the bell is ringing again, in the most self-important way.

A little later, the inspector barks to a taxi-driver: 'Gastinne-Renette, the gunsmith.'

So over a period of three days, feeling that her every move was being watched, that the house and the garden were about to be searched with a fine-tooth comb, Félicie has kept the revolver on her person! He pictures her in the front seat of the van. The road is not yet quiet enough. Maybe the vehicle is being followed. Louvet would notice if she . . . Wait for Paris . . .

At Porte Maillot, an inspector picks up her trail. To give herself time to think she goes into a cake shop, where she stuffs herself full of cream cakes. And a glass of port . . . Perhaps she doesn't like port but it ranks as one of the rare, rich things like the grapes and champagne which she took to the hospital . . . . Make for the Métro . . . Not enough people about at this time of day . . . . She waits . . . The inspector is there. He never takes his eyes off her.

Eventually six o'clock comes round. People crowd on to the trains. The passengers are packed close together . . . The heaven-sent overcoat with the gaping pockets.

Such a shame that Félicie cannot see Maigret as the taxi ferries him to the expert gunsmith. If, perhaps for the space of a second, she could forget the scares and panics, would she feel a sense of pride as she reads the admiration in the inspector's expression?

6. Maigret Stays Put

How many million times has he trudged heavily up the wide, dusty staircase of police headquarters in Quai des Orfèvres, where the wooden treads always creak faintly under the soles of his shoes and lethal draughts lurk all through winter? Maigret has some ingrained habits, one of which, for instance, consists of turning as he reaches the last few steps and looking back down the stairwell behind him. Another, when he starts plodding along the high, wide corridor of the Police Judiciaire, requires him to glance casually into what he calls the *lantern*. Situated to the left of the staircase, it is actually the glass-walled waiting room. Inside are a table covered with green cloth, green armchairs and on the walls black frames containing in small round mounted photographs of policemen who have died in the line of duty.

The lantern is crowded, although it is already five in the afternoon. Maigret is so preoccupied that for a moment he forgets that these people are here because they are part of his inquiries. He recognizes several faces. Someone bears down on him.

'Ah, inspector! How much longer is this going to take? Isn't there any way of jumping the queue?'

The cream of Place Pigalle is assembled here, summoned at his order by one of his inspectors.

'You know me, don't you? You know I'm going straight and that I wouldn't get myself mixed up in anything like this. I already wasted the afternoon . . .'

Maigret, broad-backed, walks away. As he goes he nudges open, seemingly by accident, two or three of the doors which line up as far as the eye can see. He reigns supreme at Quai des Orfèvres, which he knows like the back of his hand. Interviews are taking place in every available space, even in his own office, where Rondonnet, a new man, is sitting in Maigret's own chair, smoking a pipe that looks exactly like his. He has carried imitation to the point of having beers sent up from the Brasserie Dauphine. In the hot seat is a waiter from the Pelican. Rondonnet winks at Maigret, abandons his informant for a moment and joins the inspector in the corridor, where so many scenes like this have been enacted.

'There's something going on, sir. I'm not yet sure what exactly. You know how it works . . . I'm deliberately letting them stew in the lantern. I've a feeling they're all sticking to the same story. They know something . . . Have you seen the commissioner? Apparently he's been trying to get hold of you by phone for the last hour . . . Oh, by the way, there's a message here for you . . .'

He goes back inside and looks on the desk. It's from Madame Maigret.

Élise has just arrived from Épinal with her husband and the children. We'll all be eating together here, at home. Do try to be back. They've brought mushrooms.

Maigret won't be there. His mind is elsewhere. He is anxious to try out an idea which he had earlier while waiting for the results of the ballistics tests carried out on the premises of Monsieur Gastinne-Renette. He was walking up and down in a basement, marking time in one of the shooting galleries where a young couple – newlyweds – who were about to embark on their honeymoon in Africa were trying out various kinds of fearsome guns.

Once more he was transported back to Pegleg's house. Once again he was – mentally – climbing up the polished stairs when, still in his head, he suddenly paused on the landing, hesitated between the two doors and then remembered that there were three rooms.

'Good God!'

After that he was in an even greater hurry to get back to where he was almost certain he would make a breakthrough. He already knew what the result of the ballistics test would be: he was sure that old Lapie had been killed by the gun he had recovered in Avenue de Wagram. A Smith & Wesson. Not a toy. Not the kind of gun bought by amateurs, but a serious weapon, the tool of the professional.

A quarter of an hour later, old Monsieur Gastinne-Renette himself confirmed his theory.

'Absolutely right, detective chief inspector. I'll send you a detailed report this evening, with enlargements of the photographs.'

Even so, Maigret had wanted to call in at Quai des Orfèvres to make sure that nothing new had turned up.

Now he knocks on the commissioner's baize door and enters.

'Ah! There you are, Maigret! I was beginning to be afraid of not reaching you by phone. Was it you who sent Dunan to Rue Lepic?'

Maigret had forgotten all about this. Yes, it was. To be on the safe side. He sent Dunan to do a thorough search of Jacques Pétillon's room at the Hôtel Beauséjour.

'He phoned in earlier. It seems that someone got there before him. He wanted to see you as soon as possible. Are you going over there?'

Maigret nods. He is heavy, sullen. He hates the idea that the thread of his thoughts is about to be interrupted. Those thoughts centre on Jeanneville, not Rue Lepic.

As he emerges from the Police Judiciaire, yet another man runs after him, one of those corralled in the glass cage.

'Isn't there some way I can be seen now? I've arranged to meet someone . . .'

He shrugs his shoulders.

Not long after this, a taxi drops him in Place Blanche. As he is about to get out on to the pavement, he suddenly loses his momentum. The square is brimming with sunshine. The terrace of a large café is alive with customers, and it is as if people have nothing better to do than sit at tables, drink cool beer or aperitifs and allow their eyes to linger on all the pretty women who pass by.

For a moment, Maigret envies them. He thinks of his wife, who is at this moment being reunited with her sister and brother-in-law in their apartment in Avenue Richard

Lenoir. He thinks of the mushrooms simmering gently, giving off an aroma of garlic and damp forest. He loves mushrooms.

He too would like to sit down at the terrace of that café. He hasn't slept enough these last few nights, he's been snatching odd meals, drinking indiscriminately, always on the hoof, and has the feeling that the damned job he has chosen to do makes him live other people's lives instead of quietly living his own. Fortunately in a few years he will be able to retire. Then he will wear a large straw hat, cultivate his garden, a garden as manicured as old Lapie's, with a wine store to which he will wend his way from time to time and take a cooling draught.

'Give me a beer, and make it quick.'

He hardly takes time to sit down. He sees Inspector Dunan, who has been watching out for him.

'I've been waiting for you, sir. You've got to see . . .'

Back *there*, Félicie is most likely cooking her supper on the gas stove, with the kitchen door open to the vegetable patch now gilded by the rays of the setting sun.

He strides into the lobby of the Hôtel Beauséjour, which is squeezed between a pork-butcher's and a shoe shop. In the office, behind a small window, an enormously fat man is sitting in a Louis XV elbow chair next to the key rack, with his dropsical legs soaking in an enamel bucket.

'I can assure you it wasn't my fault. If you don't believe me, you can check with Ernest. He's the one who showed them up.'

Ernest, the porter, is even more in need of sleep than Maigret, for he works both nights and days, rarely sleeping more than two hours at a stretch. He explains in a drawling voice:

'It was early in the afternoon. At that time of day, we only get the *drop-ins*, if you take my meaning. All the rooms on the first floor are set aside for the trade. Usually we know all the girls. As they walk past they call out:

'"Going up to number 8 . . ."

'And when they come down they get their percentage, because we give them a cut of one franc on the room . . .

'Now, as I said at the time, I didn't know that one. Brunette, not too shop-soiled. She waited in the corridor to be given a key.'

'What about the man who was with her?' asks Maigret.

'Couldn't say. We don't look too closely, you know, because they don't like it. Most of the time they're a bit shy. Some deliberately look away or pretend to be wiping their noses; in winter they turn up the collars of their overcoats. He was just like all the rest. I didn't notice anything special about him. I showed them up to number 5, which was free.'

A couple pass by. A voice says:

'Number 9 all right, Ernest?'

The old man with the dropsical legs checks the key rack and replies with an affirmative growl.

'That's Jaja. She's a regular . . . What was I saying? . . . Oh yes. The man came down first after about a quarter of an hour. It's almost always the same. I didn't see the woman leave and ten minutes later at most I went up to the room, which was empty, and tidied it up . . .

'"She must have gone without me noticing," I said to myself.

'But just then a lot of clients arrived, and I thought no more about it. It was a good half-hour later that I was amazed to see the woman walk out behind my back.

'"Hello!" I said to myself. "Where's she been, then?"'

'Then I forgot all about it until your inspector, who asked for the key to the musician's room, came and started asking questions.'

'You say you'd never seen her before?'

'No, I can't say that. She wasn't a regular, that's for sure. But I had a feeling I'd come across her somewhere. Her face wasn't entirely new to me.'

'How long have you worked at the Hôtel Beauséjour?'

'Five years.'

'So she could have been an old customer?'

'It's possible. There've been so many come through that door, you know! You see them for a fortnight or a month, then they move to another neighbourhood or out of town altogether unless your lot don't cart them off first.'

A heavy-footed Maigret climbs the stairs with Inspector Dunan. Up on the fifth floor, where Pétillon lived, the lock in the door hasn't been forced. It's a basic lock and the simplest skeleton-key would make short work of it.

Looking around him, Maigret gives a whistle of surprise, for as thorough jobs go, this is a thorough job. There might not be much in the way of furniture, but it can safely be said that every inch of it has been painstakingly searched. Pétillon's grey suit is on the bedside rug with the pockets turned inside out, every drawer gapes, underwear has been scattered everywhere and the visitor has taken a pair of scissors to the mattress, pillow and eiderdown, so that floccules of wool and feathers form a layer of what looks like snow on the carpet.

'What do you reckon, sir?'

'Any prints?'

'The crew from Criminal Records has already been. I took the liberty of phoning them. They sent Moers, but he didn't find anything. What were the people who turned the place over like this looking for?'

That is not what interests Maigret. What they were after, as Dunan using the plural, expressed it, is much less important than the frenzied way they went about looking for it. They also did it without putting a foot wrong!

The revolver which killed Jules Lapie is a Smith & Wesson, a gun to be found in the pocket of every seasoned *tough guy*.

What happened after the old man died? Pétillon panics. He tours the nightclubs and the more or less unsavoury bars in Montmartre, looking for someone he does not find. Though he has a feeling the police are on his trail, he goes ahead all the same, keeps on looking, goes as far as Rouen, where he asks about a girl named Adèle, who hadn't worked in the Tivoli brasserie for several months.

This is when he loses heart. He is at the end of his tether. Maigret knows he is ripe for plucking: he'll talk . . .

And at exactly that point, he is coolly mown down in the street, and whoever pulled the trigger is no choir-boy.

He's also probably the same man who, wasting no time, hurries off to Jeanneville.

In Place Pigalle, Pétillon was standing next to Maigret, but that did not stop his assailant.

Lapie's house is being watched. The man must know, or at least suspect it, but that doesn't stop him either. He gets into the bedroom, puts a chair in front of the wardrobe and prises one of its boards loose.

Did he find what he was looking for? Disturbed by Félicie, he knocks her over and vanishes, the only trace he leaves being the prints of a pair of new shoes.

It happened around three or four o'clock in the morning. And the very next afternoon Pétillon's room was ransacked.

This time, it was a woman. A brunette and good-looking, like the Adèle who had worked in the brasserie. She does not make any mistakes. She might have got into the hotel, which was well used to the *drop-in* trade, to use the porter's word, either with her lover or an accomplice. But how can anyone tell if the Hôtel Beauséjour is not also under surveillance? She plays it straight. It is with a man she has just picked up that she asks for a room. But when he has gone, she takes to the stairs, goes up to the fifth floor – there's no one about on the upper floors at this time of day – and searches the room meticulously.

What emerges from these increasingly rushed comings and goings? That *they're* in a hurry. That *they* need to find something as soon as they can. Ergo *they* haven't found it yet.

Which is why Maigret also feels a feverish need for haste.

True, he has the same feeling every time he puts any distance between himself and Cape Horn, as if he were expecting some catastrophe to happen in his absence.

He removes the rubber band around his notebook and tears out a sheet.

Big round-up tonight, ninth and eighteenth arrondissements

'Give this to Inspector Piaulet. He'll understand.'

Back out on the street, his eye again lingers over the terrace of the café, where all people have to do is enjoy life and breathe in the spring air. What the hell! Another quick beer. His close-cut moustache still flecked with froth, he sinks into the back seat of a taxi.

'Poissy first . . . and I'll tell you from there . . .'

He struggles to stay awake. With his eyes half-closed, he vows that when the case is solved, he will sleep for twenty-four hours. He pictures his room, window wide open, the play of sunshine on the counterpane, the familiar household noises, Madame Maigret moving about on tiptoe and saying sh! to noisy delivery men.

But that, as the song goes, is what never happens for you. You go on dreaming, you promise yourself you'll live that dream, you swear it, and then, when the moment comes, the damned phone rings, even though Madame Maigret would like to strangle it, like some evil monster.

'Hello? . . . Speaking . . .'

And Maigret is off again!

'Where to now, sir?'

'Go up the slope, on the left. I'll tell you where to stop.'

His impatience returns despite his drowsiness. It's all he has thought about since his visit to Gastinne-Renette. Why didn't he think of it sooner? But he was getting very warm, as they say in children's guessing games. At first, the business with the three bedrooms had struck him. Then he had been diverted. He had been deflected by his theory about jealousy.

'On the right . . . Yes. The third house along . . . Listen, I'd like you to stay here all night. Have you eaten? . . . No? . . . Wait a minute . . . Lucas! Come here, would you? . . . Anything happened? Is Félicie there? . . . What was that? . . . She asked you in for a coffee and a glass of brandy? . . . Of course not! You're wrong. It's not because she's afraid. It's because this morning I told off a silly nurse who was sniggering at her. Her gratitude to me has rebounded on you, that's all. Make the most of the car. Go to the Anneau d'Or. Have dinner. And see to it the driver gets his. Stay in contact with the woman in the post office. Say she can expect to be disturbed tonight by the phone . . . Is the bike here?'

'I saw it in the garden leaning against the wall of the wine store.'

Félicie is watching from the doorway. When the taxi drives off and Maigret walks towards her, she asks, with her mistrust renewed:

'So you went to Paris *after all*?'

He knows what she is thinking. She is wondering if he went back to the restaurant where they'd had lunch, if he succeeded in tracing the man with grey hair, the overcoat and the muffler, and if the man has talked despite her sorry little note.

'Come with me, Félicie. This is not the time for playing games.'

'Where are you going?'

'Upstairs. Come on.'

He opens the door to old Lapie's bedroom.

'Think before you answer . . . When Jacques had this room for several months, what items of furniture, what things were in it?'

She wasn't expecting this question and she has to think. She looks round the room.

'First there was the brass bedstead which is now in the lumber room. What I mean when I say lumber room is the room next to mine, the one I was in for those few months. Since then we've used it as a dump for everything that's cluttering up the house and in the autumn we even store apples there.'

'The bed . . . And a . . . What else? . . . The washstand?'

'No. It was the same one.'

'The chairs?'

'Wait. There were chairs with leather seats, which we took down to the dining room.'

'The wardrobe?'

He has kept the wardrobe until last and he is so tense that his teeth bite hard the stem of his pipe, cracking the vulcanite stem.

'It was the same one.'

He is suddenly deflated. He feels that since his visit to Gastinne-Renette he has been in a furious hurry only to be brought up short by a blank wall, or even worse, a vacuum.

'When I say it was the same, it was the same, though not really. There are two identical wardrobes in the house. They were bought at an auction three, maybe four years ago, I can't remember which. I wasn't best pleased because I would rather have had wardrobes with mirrors. In the whole house there isn't a mirror where you can get a full view of yourself.'

Phew! If only she knew what a load she has just taken off his mind! He loses interest in her. He rushes into her room, through which he passes like a whirlwind, enters the room beyond, the one turned into a lumber room, opens the window and savagely flings open the slatted shutters, which were fully closed.

Why hadn't it occurred to him before? There is everything in this room: a roll of linoleum, old mats, chairs stacked on top of each other the way they are in a brasserie after hours. There are racks of deal shelves which are probably used for storing apples in winter, a chest containing an old Japy hand-pump, two tables and lastly, behind all this jumble of junk, a wardrobe like the one in the old man's room. Maigret is in such a hurry that he knocks over the disassembled sections of the brass bed which lean against a wall. He moves one of the tables, clambers on to it and runs his hand through the thick layer of dust on the other side of the frieze running round the top of the wardrobe.

'You don't have some sort of tool I could use?'

'What sort of tool?'

'Screwdriver, chisel, pincers, anything . . .'

Dust settles on his hair. Félicie has gone downstairs. He hears her walk across the garden and go into the wine store. She finally reappears holding a cold chisel and a hammer.

'What are you trying to do?'

Remove the slats from the back! Actually, it's not too difficult. One of them is almost loose. Underneath, he feels paper. Maigret takes hold of it and soon works free a packet wrapped in an old newspaper.

He looks down at Félicie and sees that she has gone quite pale and stiff as she raises her eyes to him.

'What's in the packet?'

'Not the faintest idea!'

She has rediscovered her sharp voice and that disdainful look.

He climbs down off the table.

'We'll soon find out, won't we? You're sure you don't know?'

Does he believe her? Or doesn't he? It is as if he's playing a game of cat and mouse. He takes his time, examines the paper before unwrapping it

'It's a newspaper and it's over a year old . . . Aha! . . . Did you know, Félicie, there were such riches in the house?'

Because what he is holding is a wad of one-thousand-franc notes.

'Hands off! No touching!'

He climbs back on to the table, removes all the slats from the top of the wardrobe and makes sure that nothing else is hidden there.

'We'll be more comfortable downstairs. Come on.'

He is jubilant. He sits down at the kitchen table. Maigret has always had a weakness for kitchens which are always full of wholesome smells and the sight of appetizing eatables: fresh vegetables, fresh meat oozing blood, chickens being plucked. The decanter from which Félicie offered a glass to Lucas is still there, and he helps himself before he starts counting the notes like some conscientious cashier.

'Two hundred and ten . . . eleven . . . twelve . . . ah, here are two stuck together . . . thirteen . . . . fourteen . . . Two hundred and twenty three, four . . . seven . . . eight . . .'

He looks at her. Her eyes are glued to the notes; all the colour has drained from her face, where the traces of where she was hit in the night now show up more clearly.

'Two hundred and twenty-nine thousand francs, Félicie . . . Well, what do you make of that? Two hundred and twenty-nine thousand francs in notes hidden in the bedroom of your boyfriend, Pétillon . . .

'Because you do realize that it was in his room that the money was hidden, don't you? The man who now has such an urgent need of the money knew exactly where it was. There was just one thing he never suspected: that there were two wardrobes. How could he know that, when Lapie went back to occupying his room, he carried his obsessions to the point of taking his own wardrobe with him and consigning the other one to the lumber room?'

'Does that leave you any further forwards?' she asks archly.

'At least it explains why you were hit so hard last night that you might have been knocked out and why, only a few hours later, your friend Jacques' room in Rue Lepic was ransacked.'

He stands up. He needs to stretch his legs. His triumph is not complete. But one success leads to another. Now that he has found what he was looking for and that his theory has been borne out by the facts – he is mentally transported back to Gastinne-Renette's shooting range where the notion had suddenly come to him! – now that he has moved forwards one square, other questions arise. He walks up and down in the garden, straightens the stem of a rose-bush, absently gathers up the dibble which Lapie, alias Pegleg, had put down shortly before going indoors to die so mindlessly in his bedroom.

Through the open kitchen window, he can see Félicie looking as if she has been turned to stone. A faint smile crosses the inspector's lips. Why not? It is as if he is saying to himself, with a shrug of his shoulders:

'Why not give it a try?'

Toying with the dibble, which still has soil clinging to it, he starts talking to her through the window.

'You know, Félicie, I'm becoming more and more convinced, surprising as it might seem, that Jacques Pétillon did not kill his uncle and even that he had nothing whatsoever to do with this entire murderous business . . .'

She stares at him without reacting in any way. Her face, tired and drawn, registers no sign of relief.

'Well, what do you say? You must be pleased.'

She does her best to oblige, but what flickers on her thin lips is a sorry, meagre smile.

'Yes, pleased. I'm grateful . . .'

And he has to make an effort not to show how pleased he is too.

'Yes, I can see that you're happy, very happy . . . And I think that now you're going to help me prove the innocence of the young man you love. Because you do love him, don't you?'

She looks away, probably so that he won't see her mouth, which betrays how close she is to tears.

'Of course you love him. There's no shame in that. I'm sure he'll mend, that you'll fall into each other's arms and that, to thank you for everything you did for him . . .'

'I've done nothing for him . . .'

'Come now! . . . But no matter. I tell you I'm quite sure that you'll marry him and raise a large family . . .'

She explodes, just as he was expecting. Isn't this exactly what he was angling for?

'You're a brute! A brute! You are the cruellest, the most . . . the most . . .'

'Because I tell you that Jacques is innocent?'

These simple words puncture her rage. She realizes she has made a mistake, but it's too late now, and she is at a loss for what to say, she is miserable and floundering helplessly.

'You know that it isn't what you really think. You're trying to make me talk. From the moment you first set foot in this house . . .'

'When did you last see Pétillon?'

But she still has enough presence of mind to say:

'This morning.'

'Before that?'

She does not answer, and Maigret makes a great show of turning round to look at the garden and the arbour with the green-painted table on which, one fine morning, there was a decanter of brandy with two liqueur glasses. Her eyes follow the direction of his. She knows what he is thinking.

'I won't say anything.'

'I know. You've told me that a dozen times at least. It's starting to sound like some old refrain. Fortunately we've recovered the banknotes . . .'

'Why fortunately?'

'You see, you're beginning to take an interest . . . When Pétillon left Cape Horn a year ago, he had fallen out with his uncle, correct?'

'They didn't get on, but . . .'

'Which is why he hasn't been back since . . .'

She tries to work out where he intends to lead her this time. Her mental effort is almost palpable.

'And in all that time you never saw him once!' Maigret muses casually. 'Or more exactly, you didn't speak to him. Otherwise you'd surely have told him that the furniture had been moved around.'

She senses danger: it is there, hidden beneath these insidious questions. God, how hard it is to defend yourself against this unflappable man who smokes his pipe and smothers you with that fatherly eye! She hates him! Yes, loathes him! No one has ever caused her as much pain as this inspector who will not let her alone for a moment and says the most unexpected things in that same, even voice while he pulls gently on his pipe.

'You weren't his mistress, were you, Félicie . . .'

Should she agree or should she deny it? What is he trying to make her say?

'If you were his mistress, you would have seen him again, because the quarrel with his uncle had nothing to do with the way you felt about him. You would have had an opportunity to tell him that the old man had moved back to his old room. That way, Pétillon would have known that the piggy-bank wasn't in his old room but with the rest of the junk. Now listen carefully . . . Knowing that, he wouldn't have broken into the bedroom, where, God only knows why, he'd been forced to kill his uncle . . .'

'It's not true . . .'

'Therefore, you weren't his mistress.'

'No . . .'

'Did you ever sleep with him?'

'No . . .'

'Did he know you were in love with him?'

'No.'

Maigret allows a satisfied smile to spread over his face.

'Well now, girl, that, I think, is the first time you haven't lied to me since the start of this investigation . . . Look, I knew all about this love affair of yours from the start. You're a girl whose life hasn't exactly been showered with good things. So in the absence of solid realities, you wove your own reality out of your dreams. You stopped being young Félicie, old man Lapie's housekeeper, and became all the glamorous heroines in those novels you read.

'In your dreams, Pegleg wasn't just a pernickety old man you worked for but, as in the best novelettes, you became a child conceived in sin . . . No need for blushes . . . You craved drama, if only to impress your friend Léontine, but also so you could write it down in your diary.

'So when a man came to live in the house, you told yourself that you were his mistress, you became the heroine of a love story, and I'm pretty sure the poor boy never suspected a thing . . . And I'm equally sure that Forrentin, the estate manager, never gave you a second glance, and that it was that goatee of his that helped you to turn him into a satyr.'

For a moment, a fleeting smile appears on Félicie's lips. But then it is gone and she becomes spiteful again.

'Where is all this leading?'

He is frank:

'I don't know yet, but I will soon, and it will all be due to the parcel of notes we found . . . Now I'm going to ask you something. The people who are looking for the money and need it so badly that they are prepared to run all the risks they have taken since yesterday aren't going to give up at this stage of the game. What I worked out, the fairly obvious conclusion about the furniture being moved round, they could work out too. I'd rather you weren't here alone tonight. Hate me if you like, but I must ask you to let me stay the night in the house. You can lock yourself in your room . . . What are you having for dinner?'

'Black pudding. I was about to start making the mashed potato.'

'Excellent. Invite me. I've just got to go down to Orgeval and give few instructions and I'll come back. Agreed?'

'If you insist.'

'Smile!'

'No.'

He stuffs the banknotes in his pocket, then retrieves the bike, which is parked outside the wine store. He makes the most of the opportunity to pour himself a glass, and just as he is getting into the saddle she calls out:

'I still hate you!'

He turns with a smile:

'And I adore you, Félicie!'

7. The Night of the Lobster

Six thirty in the evening. It is approximately the time when, outside Cape Horn, Maigret gets on his bike and turns round with his parting shot to Félicie, who is standing in the door of the house:

'And I adore you, Félicie!'

In Béziers, the ringing of the telephone echoes through the police station. The front window is wide open. The office is empty. Arsène Vadibert, the station chief's secretary, who is outside in his shirtsleeves watching a game of boules under the plane trees, turns towards the barred window, where the phone continues to ring insistently and malevolently.

'I'm coming! I'm coming!' he cries reluctantly.

And still in his strong Midi accent he mutters: 'Hold your horses.'

'Hello? . . . Is that Paris? . . . Speak up! . . . What? . . . This is Béziers . . . Béziers, yes, as it is written . . . Police Judiciaire? . . . We got your request . . . I said we received your request . . . Don't you speak French in Paris? . . . Your request concerning a woman called Adèle . . . It so happens we might just have what you're looking for . . .'

He leans forwards a little so that he has a clear view of his white-shirted, pock-faced friend, who is lining up for an onslaught on an opponent's boule.

'It happened last week, Thursday, at the house . . . What was that? . . . Which house? . . . The whorehouse. . . . It's called the Paradou . . . Girl called Adèle, small, dark hair . . . What? . . . Breasts like pears? . . . That I couldn't tell you, no sir . . . I never saw them myself . . . Anyway, she's gone away . . . If you'd only listen you'd know already . . . I got other things to do . . . I'm telling you this girl called Adèle wanted to move on and asked to be paid what was owed her. The madam called the owner. Seems she couldn't just walk out like that, she had to work to the end of the month, so he wouldn't give her what she said was owing, so she smashed bottles, tore up cushions, kicked up one hell of a shindig, in the end, since she didn't have any money, she borrowed some from another girl and walked out anyway . . . Went to Paris . . . How? . . . Haven't a clue . . . You asked about Adèle and I'm giving you one . . . Not at all, 'bye . . .'

Six thirty-five. The Anneau d'Or at Orgeval. An open door in the middle of the greyish-white frontage. A bench on either side of the door. A laurel bush in a sawn-down wine barrel at the end of each. The benches and the half-barrels are painted dark green. The line between shade and sun bisects the pavement exactly. A van pulls up. The butcher gets out. He is wearing an overall patterned with small blue checks.

Inside, in the bar, it is cool and shady. The landlord is playing cards with Forrentin, Lepape and the driver of the taxi which brought Maigret. Lucas looks on, smoking his pipe with a composure borrowed from his boss. The landlord's wife is washing glasses. The butcher comes in:

'Evening all! A large glass of the white, Jeanne. Listen, fancy a nice fresh lobster? I was given two in town, and at home there's only me that eats them because the wife reckons lobster brings her out in a rash . . .'

He goes out to get the lobster, which is still alive, from his van. He comes back, holding it by one claw. Then a window opens across the road, a hand waves, and a voice sings out:

'Phone, Monsieur Lucas!'

'Before you go, tell me, Monsieur Lucas. Do you like lobster?'

Does he like lobster!

'Germaine! Make us up a stock! For cooking a lobster.'

'Hello? . . . Yes, Lucas . . . The chief isn't very far . . . Say again? Béziers? . . . Adèle . . . Last Thursday? . . .'

Maigret gets off his bike just as the butcher drives off. He watches the card game while Lucas is still on the phone. The lobster crawls clumsily across the stone-flagged floor, along the front of the counter

'Tell me, madame, is that lobster yours? Do you really want it?'

'I was just about to cook it. I thought it would do for your sergeant and the taxi-driver.'

'They can have something else. I'll take it off your hands, if it's all right with you.'

Lucas walks back across the street.

'They've come up with an Adèle, sir. In Béziers. She left in a hurry on Thursday and travelled to Paris.'

From time to time, the card-players give them the odd glance and listen and catch snippets of their conversation.

*

Ten minutes to seven. Inspector Rondonnet and Chief Inspector Piaulet are talking in an office of the Police Judiciaire. Tall windows look down on the Seine, where a tug is straining hard.

'Hello? . . . Is that Orgeval? . . . Operator, would you be good enough to ask Detective Chief Inspector Maigret to come to the phone?'

The same hand again waves out of the window. Lucas runs across the road. Maigret, the lobster in one hand, is just about to mount his bike.

'It's for you, sir.'

'Hello? . . . That you Piaulet? . . . Anything new?'

'Rondonnet thinks he's come up with something . . . According to the doorman at the Sancho, which is just over the road from the Pelican, the club's owner went out last night while you were there and phoned from the bar on the corner . . . Hello? . . . Yes, still here . . . A little later, a taxi pulled up. No one got out of it. The owner, keeping his voice down, talked to somebody inside . . . Are you with me? . . . There's some funny business there . . . Also, on Saturday evening, an argument broke out in the tobacconist's in Rue Fontaine . . . Hard to know exactly . . . It involved a dubious character . . .'

'Ouch!' growls Maigret.

'What?'

'Oh nothing. It's the lobster . . . I'm listening . . .'

'That's about it, really. We're continuing to interview the ones we rounded up. Some seem to know more than they're saying . . .'

'My turn now . . . Hello? . . . Check records . . . A report,

I don't know, a break-in or similar, maybe fraud or false pretences, about thirteen months ago. Find out who in the Place Pigalle sector was living at that time with a girl called Adèle . . . You can phone any time tonight . . . Lucas will stay near the phone . . . What is it?'

'Just a moment . . . Rondonnet's listening on the extension, he's saying something . . . I'll pass him on to you . . .'

'Hello, is that you, chief? I don't know if this is relevant. It suddenly came back to me because the date is right. In April last year. I dealt with it. Rue Blanche, do you remember? Pedro, who owned the Chamois . . .'

Since the lobster won't stay still, Maigret carefully puts it on the floor and growls at it:

'Stay there!'

'What?'

'Talking to the lobster . . . Pedro . . . Remind me . . .'

'A small club in Rue Blanche on the lines of the Pelican, but raunchier . . . Tall and thin, always looked pale, had a white streak, just the one, running through his black hair . . .'

'I'm with you . . .'

'It was three in the morning. He was about to close. A car stopped outside, five men got out, left the engine running, walked in, barged past the head waiter, who was already putting up the shutters . . .'

'I remember vaguely . . .'

'They manhandled Pedro into a small room behind the bar. A few minutes later there was gunfire, mirrors were shattered, bottles were thrown, then suddenly all the lights went out. I was on duty in the neighbourhood. It was a miracle that we arrived in time to nab four of the gang, including Legs, who'd hidden on the roof . . . Pedro was dead, with four or five bullets in him. Only one of the murderers got away, and it was a good few days before we found out that it was a musician, Albert Babeau. He was the one they called Shorty because he was really small and wore heels to make himself look taller . . . Just a moment . . . Chief Inspector Piaulet is telling me something . . . No . . . He wants to speak to you himself . . . I'll pass you back to him . . .'

'Hello, Maigret . . . I remember it too . . . I have the file in my office . . . Do you want me to . . .'

'Don't bother . . . The Musician was arrested at Le Havre, it's all coming back to me now . . . How many days later? . . .'

'About a week. There was an anonymous tip-off . . .'

'How many years did he get?'

'If you need that, you'll have to contact Court Records. Cat Burglar's the one who got the stiffest sentence because there were three bullets missing from the cartridge-clip of his revolver. Twenty years he got if I remember correctly. For the rest, sentences ranged from five years to one. It was always thought that Pedro kept large sums of money at home, but none of it was ever recovered. Do you think there's a connection? . . . Look, would it help if you came back here? . . .'

Maigret hesitates. His foot accidentally nudges the lobster.

'I can't just now. Listen. This is what we'll have to do. Lucas will stay in contact all night . . .'

When he eventually comes out of the phone booth he tells the woman operating the exchange:

'I warned you that you wouldn't get much sleep tonight . . . Actually, I don't think you'll get any at all.'

Then he has a few words for Lucas, who gazes glumly at the lobster.

'Will do, sir . . . Yes, sir . . . Shall I keep the taxi on?'

'That would be safest.'

Maigret again takes to the road he has already travelled so many times in recent days, lit by a gorgeous sunset. He looks with some satisfaction at the toy houses of Jeanneville, which will soon cease to feature on his horizon and be no more than a memory.

A wholesome smell rises from the earth, the crickets begin to sing, and there is nothing more artless or more restful than vegetables growing in the neat beds by the placid retired men in straw hats who are now wielding their watering cans.

'It's me!' he cries as he walks into the hallway of Cape Horn, which is full of the smell of grilled sausage.

Holding the lobster behind his back he says:

'Say, Félicie . . . One very important question . . .'

She is immediately on the defensive.

'Do you know how to make a decent mayonnaise?'

A smile of disdain.

'Good. In that case you can make one now and put this customer on to cook . . .'

He is content. He rubs his hands. Seeing that the door to the dining room is open, he goes in but scowls when he sees that the table is laid with a red checked tablecloth, a single crystal glass, silver cutlery and an attractive bread basket, but only one place is set.

He says nothing. He waits. He is in no doubt that the lobster, which is now beginning to turn red in the boiling water, will be a never-ending source of barbed comments from his wife. Madame Maigret is not jealous, or at least she says she isn't.

'Jealous of what, for goodness' sake!' she readily exclaims with a little laugh that is not altogether natural.

But that never stops her saying again and again when they are with family or friends and the topic of Maigret's job comes up:

'It's not always as awful as people imagine . . . For example, it happens that a case can be investigated while eating lobster with a young woman named Félicie and then spending the night close to her.'

Poor Félicie! God knows she has love on the brain! She comes and goes, with that hard Norman head and solid, thrusting brow full of anxious or desperate thoughts. The coming of dusk makes her gloomy and apprehensive. Through the open window she watches Maigret walking up and down. Perhaps she wonders, like the good Lord, if this cup will ever be taken from her.

But has he not picked some flowers? He has even arranged them nicely in a vase.

'By the way, Félicie, where did poor old Lapie used to eat?'

'In the kitchen. Why? It was hardly worth making the dining room untidy just for him.'

'Quite so.'

Whereupon he moves the cutlery and the cloth and lays the table next to the gas stove while she, tense and nervous, just knows she'll ruin the mayonnaise.

'If all goes well, if you do what you're told, I might have some good news for you in the morning . . .'

'What sort of news?'

'I told you, it will have to keep until tomorrow morning!'

Though he might want to avoid being cruel to her, he cannot help himself. He may sense that she is unhappy, that she does not know which way to turn and has reached the end of her tether, but he still can't help teasing her, as if he feels the need to get his own back for something she has done.

Is this partly because he feels guilty for being here instead of directing the epic operation which is even now getting under way in the area around Place Pigalle?

'A general's place isn't in the middle of the battle!'

Point taken! But does he really have to stay so far away that he has had to devise a system of couriers and relays, mobilize the woman on the switchboard and make poor Lucas traipse from Orgeval to Jeanneville and from Jeanneville to Orgeval, as if he were some country postman?

'The man who is after the money may well work it out for himself that the furniture could have been switched round. He might also be thinking of coming back and who knows if this time he'll settle for stopping Félicie with just a punch?'

All that is perfectly reasonable, of course, but, say what you will, it is not the whole story. The truth is that Maigret finds a certain satisfaction in staying put here, in the peace-ful, almost unreal surroundings of a make-believe village, while at the same time he pulls the strings of another world that is all too real and brutal.

'Why have you moved your knife and fork in here?'

'Because I insist on eating with you. I said so when I invited myself. This is the first and probably the last time we shall have dinner together. Unless . . .'

He smiles. She says insistently:

'Unless what?'

'Forget it. We'll talk about it in the morning and if we have time we'll add up all the lies you've told . . . Take this claw . . . Oh, go on!'

And suddenly, as they eat under the kitchen light, he surprises himself thinking:

'But someone murdered Pegleg!'

Poor old Pegleg! His was a strange fate indeed! He hates adventure so much that he says no to the commonest form of adventure: marriage. But that doesn't save him from losing a leg at Cape Horn on the other side of the world, on a three-masted sailing ship!

His craving for a quiet life leads him to Jeanneville, where human passions are not allowed in, where the houses are toys, where the trees look like trees made of painted wood in children's nurseries.

But it is to this place that adventure comes looking for him once more, and it arrives breathing menace from a place where he has never set foot, a place full of horrors which he never dreamed existed, from Place Pigalle, which is inhabited by a race apart and is a kind of Parisian jungle where the tigers have slicked-down hair and carry Smith & Wessons in their pockets.

And one morning that is no different from any other morning, a morning washed with bright watercolours, he is gardening, his straw hat on his head, pricking out innocent seedlings which would yield tomatoes which he can perhaps already see in his mind, heavy and red, juicy, their thin skins bursting in the sun, and then, only minutes later, he is lying dead in his bedroom, which smells of polish and the countryside.

Just as she used to, before all this happened, Félicie sits down to eat at a corner of the table and is constantly getting up to see to a pan on the gas stove or to pour boiling water into the coffee-pot. The window is open, and in the blue of the night, which turns into velvet spangled with stars, invisible crickets call to each other, frogs take their place in the chorus, a train chugs along the valley, men play cards in the Anneau d'Or and the ever-faithful Lucas eats chops instead of lobster.

'What are you doing?'

'I'm washing up.'

'Not tonight, Félicie. You're exhausted. I would be very glad if you just went to bed . . . I insist! You must lock your door . . .'

'I'm not sleepy.'

'Really? In that case I've got something to help you to sleep. Give me half a glass of water. Two of these pills . . . There. Drink up, now. Nothing to be afraid of. I've no intention of poisoning you . . .'

She drinks, to show him that she's not afraid. As a

reaction to Maigret's paternal manner, she once more feels to the need to say:

'I still hate you. One day you'll be sorry for all the harm you've done. Anyway, tomorrow I shall be going away.'

'Where?'

'Anywhere. I don't want to see you ever again. I don't want to stay in this house, where you'll be able to do what you want.'

'Understood. Tomorrow . . .'

'Where are you going?'

'Upstairs, with you. I just want to make sure everything's all right in your room . . . Good. The shutters are closed . . . Goodnight, Félicie.'

When he comes back down to the kitchen, the carcass of the lobster is still in an earthenware dish, and there it will stay, where he can see it, all through the night.

The alarm-clock standing on the black doily on the mantelpiece is registering half past nine when he takes off his shoes, climbs the stairs noiselessly, listens and checks that Félicie, knocked out by the gardenal, is sleeping peacefully.

A quarter to ten. Maigret is sitting in Pegleg's basket chair. He is smoking his pipe. His eyes are half closed. The sound of an engine through the darkness of the fields. A car door slams. Then Lucas, who has walked into the bamboo coat stand in the dark hallway, lets rip with a choice oath.

'There was a phone call, sir . . .'

'Sh! Keep it down. She's sleeping.'

Lucas eyes the lobster with just a hint of resentment.

'The Musician was living with a woman known as Adèle.

They found her file. Her real name is Jeanne Grosbois. She was born near Moulins . . .'

'Go on.'

'At the time the Chamois was done over, she was working at the Tivoli brasserie in Rouen. She left the day after Pedro was murdered.'

'She must have gone to Le Havre with the Musician. Any more?'

'She spent a few months in Toulon, at Les Floralies, then Béziers. She made no secret of the fact that her man was in the Santé prison.'

'Has she been seen in Paris?'

'Sunday. One of her old friends spotted her in Place Clichy. She said she would be taking off for Brazil at any time soon.'

'Is that all?'

'No. The Musician was released last Friday.'

All that was what Maigret called 'in-house detective work'. Now, at precisely this moment, police vans are taking up positions in deserted sidestreets in the area around Place Pigalle. At Quai des Orfèvres, the questioning of villains, who are getting impatient and beginning to think that something serious is going on, continues.

'Phone in and tell them to send you a photo of the Musician as quick as they can. There must be one in Court Records. On second thoughts, no . . . Phone first and send the taxi to collect it.'

'Anything else, sir?'

'Yes. When the driver gets back with the photo, I want you to go to Poissy. There's a café-bar just next to the bridge. It will be closed. Wake the owner. He's an old lag. Stick the photo under his nose and ask him if it is the same man who almost got physical with Félicie at his place on Sunday evening.'

The car drives off. Once again there is silence and unbroken night. In his hand, Maigret warms the small glass of brandy which he poured himself, sips it and from time to time looks up at the ceiling.

Félicie turns over in her sleep, and the bed springs creak. What is she dreaming of? Does she have as much imagination at night as she does during the day?

Eleven o'clock. Under the eaves of the Palais de Justice, a clerk in a grey overall opens a folder and from it takes two photos with unnaturally sharp lines, one showing the full face, the other the profile. He hands them to the driver, who will deliver them to Lucas.

In the area around Place Pigalle, crowds spill out of the cinemas of Montmartre, the luminous sails of the Moulin Rouge turn above the throng, through which the buses nose their way with difficulty. Hotel porters in blue, red and green braided uniforms, bouncers and black doormen take their places outside night clubs while Detective Chief Inspector Piaulet stands in the middle of the square, keeping an eye on the unseen operation.

Janvier has stationed himself in the bar of the Pelican, an excessively dimly lit room where the band are removing the covers from their instruments. It does not escape his notice that a waiter hurries back from outside, looking scared, and hustles the owner into the cloakroom.

Side by side with the law-abiding citizens who have had

an enjoyable evening and are drinking a last beer on the terraces of the brasseries before going home to bed, the other Montmartre, the one which is just waking up, is alive with various rumours and whispers. There is a tension in the air. The owner emerges from the cloakroom, smiles at Janvier and mutters something to one of the girls who are sitting in a corner.

'I don't think I'll be staying late tonight,' she says. 'I'm tired.'

There are many like her who, ever since news of the presence of police vans has gone the rounds, do not feel any desire to hang around in this dangerous part of town. But on Boulevard Rochechouart, Rue de Douai, Rue Notre-Dame-de-Lorette and all the main routes out of the area, the men and women in uniform suddenly start seeing unobtrusive figures coming out of the dark.

'Papers . . .'

What follows depends on the mood they're in.

'On your way.'

Or more frequently:

'Get in.'

In, that is, to the prison vans, whose headlamps cast a feeble light along the pavement.

Are the Musician and Adèle still inside the trap set by the police? Will they manage to slip out through the net? But in any case, they'll know the score. And even if they have gone to ground in an attic, some helpful soul will have put them in the picture.

A quarter to midnight. Lucas, killing time playing dominoes with the landlord of the Anneau d'Or – just one light has been left on in the deserted bar – gets to his feet when he hears the taxi pull up outside.

'I'll be gone about half an hour,' he says.

Time enough to drive down to Poissy and then go back up for a few words with the chief.

The café-bar is in darkness. Lucas's knocking is loud in the still of the night. Then a woman in curlers puts her head out of a window

'Fernand! It's for you . . .'

A light goes on, footsteps, grunts, the door opens a crack.

'Eh? . . . What? . . . I just knew that business would land me in it . . . I'm licensed. I got bills to pay. I don't want to get involved . . .'

Standing by the counter in the greyish room, his braces dangling down his thighs and his hair rumpled, he stares at the two photos.

'Right . . . Well, what do you want to know?'

'Is this the man who was put in his place by Félicie?'

'And?'

'And nothing. That's it. Did you know him before Sunday?'

'Never set eyes on him until then . . . What's he done?'

Midnight. Lucas gets out of the car, and Maigret jumps in his chair like a sleeping man who is woken up. He hardly seems to be taking any interest in what the sergeant is telling him.

'I thought so.'

Dealing with villains is as easy as pie, tough as they are or think they are. They are known for it. You can say in advance exactly what they will do. But it's not the same as coping with a phenomenon like Félicie, who has given him so many headaches.

'What do I do next, sir?'

'Go back to Orgeval. Just carry on playing dominoes while you're waiting for the phone to ring.'

'How did you know I was playing dominoes?'

'Because there are only two of you, the landlord and you, and because you can't play cards.'

'Do you think anything is going to happen here?'

Maigret shrugs. He doesn't know. It doesn't matter.

'Goodnight.'

One in the morning. Félicie has started talking in her sleep. Standing outside her door, Maigret has tried to make out what she was saying, but couldn't. Without thinking, he tried the handle and the door opened slightly.

He smiles. How very sweet of her! She trusts him in spite of everything, as she hasn't locked herself in. He listens for a moment to her breathing, to the jumbled syllables which she murmurs like a child, he sees the milky patch which is the bed and the dark stain of her hair on the pillow. He shuts the door again and goes back downstairs in tiptoe.

A loud blast of a whistle in Place Pigalle. It's the signal. All exits are now covered. Uniformed men march in line, rounding up men and women who spring out of nowhere and try to get past the checkpoint. A policeman is badly bitten on the thumb by a large woman with red hair in evening dress. The police vans start filling up.

The owner of the Pelican, standing in his doorway

drawing anxiously on his cigarette, tries to complain:

'I assure you, officer, there's nothing to see inside. Just a few Americans on the town.'

Someone tugs at the jacket of the young Inspector Dunan, who had waited for Maigret that afternoon at the Hôtel Beauséjour. Ah! It's the hotel waiter. He's probably come out to see the fun.

'Quick . . . It's her!'

He points to the glazed door of a bar. The sole occupant, the owner, stands behind his bar counter. At the back, a door is just closing, but not before the inspector has had time to see the figure of a woman.

'The one who came in with the man . . .'

Adèle . . . The inspector calls up two uniformed men . . . They rush towards the door, tear through the deserted cloakroom and down a set of narrow steps, which smell of damp, stale wine and urine.

'Open up!'

They have reached the cellar. The door is locked. One of the officers breaks it down with a shoulder charge.

'Hands up whoever's in there . . .'

The beam of an electric torch lights up barrels, racks of bottles and cases of aperitifs. Nothing stirs. Or rather, when they became absolutely still, as the inspector orders his men to do, they hear a sound of short breathing, almost like the palpitations of a terrified heart.

'Stand up, Adèle.'

She leaps out in a fury from behind a pile of packing-cases and puts up a desperate struggle as if against all the odds she still hopes she can escape from the three policemen who have the devil's own job trying to get the handcuffs on her.

'Where's your boyfriend?'

'Don't know.'

'What were you doing in the street?'

'No idea.'

She sneers: 'Oh, it's a lot easier going after a defenceless woman than hunting for the Musician, isn't it?'

They grab her handbag. Back in the bar they open it and find only her battered registration card, a little loose change and some letters written in pencil, probably the letters which the Musician smuggled out of his cell to be sent to his mistress, for they were addressed to her at Béziers.

A first police van, with a full load, is driven to the cells in the Préfecture de Police, which is going to be crowded tonight. A fair number of gentlemen in dinner-jackets and ladies in evening dresses and even waiters and porters have been rounded up.

'At least we got his girlfriend, sir . . .'

Detective Chief Inspector Piaulet asks, though without great hopes:

'Are you sure you don't want to come clean? Where is he?'

'You won't find him.'

'Take her away. Not in a van. Send her to Rondonnet.'

All through the apartment blocks and furnished hotel rooms doors are being knocked on, papers are being checked, men in shirtsleeves are mortified to have been found not only where they are but found there when they are not alone.

'All I ask is that you make sure that my wife . . .'

Of course! Of course!

'Hello! Is that you, Lucas? . . . Will you tell Maigret that Adèle is here . . . Yes . . . She's not talking, of course . . . No, nothing on the Musician . . . We're continuing to question her, yes . . . We're still keeping the whole district under wraps . . .'

Now that the most of the goats have been separated from the sheep, calm has more or less returned to the area around Place Pigalle, a flat calm after the storm. The streets are quieter than usual, and the night-owls who drift up from the centre of town are very disconcerted to find the taverns so dead or to be approached by singularly unpersistent cabaret touts.

Four o'clock. It's the third time Lucas has walked into Cape Horn. Maigret has removed his collar and tie.

'You wouldn't have any tobacco on you by any chance? I smoked my last pipe an hour ago . . .'

'Adèle's behind bars.'

'What about him?'

He is afraid he might be wrong, and yet . . . The Musician is flat broke, that much is certain. Just before he was released from prison, Adèle left Béziers with hardly any money. He comes out to Poissy. That was on Sunday. Maybe he even ventured up as far as Jeanneville? He follows Félicie to the café-bar. Wouldn't the simplest plan be to seduce the maid in the cockatoo get-up? That way he could get into the house without any bother . . .

But she slaps his face!

Then the next day, which was Monday, old Lapie is killed

in his bedroom. The Musician has to get away without the wad of cash.

'What time was Adèle arrested?'

'Half an hour ago. They phoned as soon as they had her.'

'Right, off you go. Get the taxi.'

'Do you think he'll . . .'

'Get a move on. Go on.'

Maigret carefully shuts the door behind him, then sits down again in the kitchen, by the window, after turning out the light and catching yet another glimpse of the red shell of the lobster on the table.

8. *Félicie's Café au Lait*

Her eyes are wide open. She does not know what time it is. Last night she forgot to wind up her alarm-clock as she usually does. The room is filled with almost complete darkness, for all that is visible of the approaching dawn are silver streaks through the slats of the shutters.

Félicie listens. Her mind is blank. Mind and body are still sluggish, as if she has been worn down by sleeping too deeply, and for the moment she cannot tell what is real from what she has dreamed. She has been quarrelling, arguing vehemently, she has even come to blows with the placid man she hates so much who is bent on destroying her. Ah! how she loathes him!

Who opened the door? Because someone did during the night. She was lying there, waiting, worrying. It was pitch-dark. Yellowish light came in from the landing, but the door closed, and a car engine started up . . . The sound of car engines has flitted in and out of her entire night's sleep.

She does not move, she dares not move, she feels a threat of danger hanging over her. Her stomach feels heavy . . . The lobster . . . She remembers. She ate too much lobster. She took some drug. The man forced her to take a drug . . .

She strains her ears. What's that? There's someone in the kitchen. She recognizes the familiar sound of the coffee grinder. Her thoughts wander. It's not possible that anyone could be actually grinding coffee beans . . .

She stares at the ceiling, all her senses now fully alert. Boiling water is being poured. The aroma floats up the stairs and reaches her. The rattle of crockery. Another sound she knows so well: the sugar-tin being opened, the cupboard door . . .

Someone is coming upstairs. And last night she did not lock herself in, she remembers that clearly. Why didn't she just turn the key? It was pride! Yes, so that she wouldn't show the man that she was afraid. She had promised herself that she would get up quietly and do it, later, after he'd gone back down, but she had gone straight to sleep.

A knock at the door. She props herself up on one elbow. She stares at the door fearfully, her nerves are raw. The knock comes again.

'What is it?'

'Breakfast.'

Frowning hard, she looks around for her dressing gown, does not find it and quickly slips down under the bed-clothes just as the door opens, and the first thing she sees is a tray covered with a serviette and a cup with blue spots . . .

'Sleep well?'

It's Maigret, more placid than ever. He doesn't seem to realize that he is in a young woman's bedroom and that she is still in bed.

'What do you want with me?'

He puts the tray down on the small table. He is wide awake and in fine fettle. Where did he wash and shave?

Downstairs, obviously. In the kitchen, or maybe the lip of the well. His hair is still damp.

'I assume it's café au lait that you like in the morning? Unfortunately, I wasn't able to leave the house and go round to Madame Chochoi's for fresh bread . . . Eat up, girl . . . Do you want me to turn round so you can put this dressing gown on?'

She obeys unwillingly and drinks a mouthful of very hot coffee, then becomes still, the action of her hands temporarily suspended.

'Who's downstairs?'

Someone moved, she is sure of it.

'Who is downstairs? Answer me.'

'The murderer.'

'What did you say?'

She has flung off the bedclothes.

'What scheming trickery are you up to now? You vowed you'd drive me mad. And I have no one to defend me, no one to . . .'

He sits on the edge of the bed. He watches while she rants on wildly, shakes his head and sighs:

'Listen, I'm telling you that the man downstairs is the murderer. I knew he'd come back. Given the fix he was in, he had to risk everything. Besides which, he very likely thought I'd be in Paris, directing operations there. It didn't occur to him that I was determined to keep a close watch on the house.'

'You mean he came?'

She pulls herself together. She is all at sea. Seizing Maigret by the wrists, she cries:

'Who . . . Who is he? How is it possible that . . .'

She is so eager to know the answer that she rushes out on to the stairs, intending go down and see for – and by – herself, slim and uneasy in her vivid blue dressing gown, but stops, overcome by fear.

'Who is he?'

'Do you still hate me?'

'Yes . . . I don't know . . .'

'Why did you lie to me?'

'Because!'

'Listen to me, Félicie . . .'

'I won't listen to you any more . . . I'm going to open the window and scream for help.'

'Why did you never tell me that when you got back here on Monday morning you saw Jacques Pétillon actually coming out of the garden? Because you did see him. He was walking away behind the hedge. It was for him that old Lapie fetched the decanter and two glasses from the sideboard. He thought his nephew had come to make peace, ask to be forgiven, something along those lines.'

She stares at him, stony-faced, without moving, unprotesting.

'And you thought it was Jacques who killed his uncle. You found the gun in the bedroom and you kept it on you for three days before getting rid of it by slipping it into the pockets of a man on the Métro. You imagined you were a heroine risking all to save the man you loved – though the poor devil never suspected a thing. So it was because of you and your lies that he was almost arrested for a murder he did not commit . . .'

'How do you know all this?'

'Because the actual murderer is downstairs.'

'Who is he?'

'You don't know him.'

'You're still trying to make me say things. I'm not going to answer any more of your questions, do you hear? I won't tell you anything else. For a start, you can get out of here and let me get dressed . . . No . . . Stay . . . Why did Jacques come back on Monday morning?'

'Because Mr Music had asked him to.'

'Mr Music?'

'A friend of his. In Paris people make acquaintances of all sorts, you know, some good, some bad . . . Especially if you play the saxophone in a night club . . . You'd better drink your coffee while it is still lukewarm . . .'

He opens the shutters and looks out of the window.

'Ah! There's your friend Léontine, she's going for the bread . . . She's looking this way . . . What a lot of tales you'll have to tell her now!'

'I shan't be telling her anything!'

'Want to bet?'

'I wouldn't bet with you.'

'Do you still hate me as much?'

'Is Jacques innocent?'

'If he is, you'll stop hating me. If he isn't, then it will be the opposite . . . Oh really, Félicie! . . . Actually Jacques is guilty because one evening, just over a year ago, when he was living here in this house, under his uncle's roof, guilty, I say, of letting a certain person stay here for one or more nights, someone he'd met in Montmartre . . . A man named Albert Babeau, known as the Musician and also called Shorty, who ran girls . . .'

'Ran girls?'

'You wouldn't understand. He was being hunted by the police for his part in the Chamois shooting. He remembered his pal Pétillon, who was then living with an elderly uncle in the country . . . A good place to hide up for a villain who was being sought by the police.'

'I remember . . .' she says suddenly.

'Remember what?'

'The only time Jacques . . . The only times he was ever rude to me . . . I'd gone into his room without knocking. I just had time to hear sounds, as if something was being hidden.'

'Actually it was the sound of someone being hidden or maybe taking cover, someone who shouldn't have been there. And before moving on, that someone thought it would be a good idea to hide his loot in the room and loosened a board for it on top of the wardrobe. Later he was caught. He served a year in prison . . . Why are you looking at me like that?'

'No reason . . . Go on.'

She blushes, then looks away. Although she did not know it, she had been gazing at the inspector in admiration.

'When he got out he was broke and he naturally thought about his money. His first idea was to cosy up to you, which would have been a very convenient way of getting inside the house . . .'

'Me? You can't think for one moment that I'd . . .'

'But you slapped his face for him. So he went looking

for Pétillon, he told him some yarn or other, that he'd left something important here, that he needed his help to come and get it . . . While Jacques was talking to old man Lapie in the garden . . .'

'I understand . . .'

'And none too soon.'

'Thanks a lot!'

'Think nothing of it . . . Pegleg must have heard a noise. He must have had pretty good hearing.'

'Too good!'

'He went up to his room, and the Musician, disturbed just as he was climbing on to a chair, panicked and put a bullet in him . . . Alarmed by the noise of the gun, Pétillon fled in one direction, and the murderer made off in the other . . . You saw Jacques, your own, your very own Jacques but you didn't see the Musician, who left by another way . . .

'And that was it. Obviously Jacques didn't say anything. When he felt that suspicion was falling on him he panicked, like the kid he is . . .'

'That's not true!'

'You don't want him to be a kid? All right, then, he's a fool. Instead of coming to me and telling what he knew, he decided to go looking for the Musician to get what was owing to him. He looked in all the shady places where he knew he could usually be found. He even went to Rouen as a last resort, to ask his mistress . . .'

'How did he know that woman?' asks Félicie, green with jealousy.

'That, Félicie, I do not know . . . In Paris, these

things . . . Anyway, he starts feeling desperate . . . He can't go on . . . Then that evening he can't stand it any longer and is about to tell what he knows when the Musician, who has been warned, takes a pot shot at him to teach him to keep his trap shut.'

'Don't talk like that . . .'

'That night, the Musician comes back here, hoping at last to get his hands on his money . . . You have no idea how difficult it is to keep one step ahead of the police when your pockets are empty . . . He finds nothing on top of the wardrobe. But he leaves you with something to remember him by . . . If the money isn't here, maybe Pétillon found it, and that's why Adèle was sent to search his room in Rue Lepic.

'It's not there either. That night, Montmartre is besieged. The Musician is cornered, like a stag at bay. Adèle is arrested . . .

'Somehow, the Musician manages to get past the police checkpoints and, more determined than ever, just as men of that type can be, he finds a taxi to take him to Poissy. He is so broke that he pays the driver with a swift blow on the back of the neck with a cosh.'

Félicie shudders. She is looking at Maigret's face as if it were a cinema screen and she was watching an exciting film.

'Did he come?'

'He came . . . Quietly, without making any noise . . . He came in through the garden without stepping on a single twig, then walked past the kitchen window, which was open . . .'

In her eyes, Maigret is already a hero. She is thrilled.

'Did you fight?'

'No. Just when he was least expecting it, he felt the unpleasant sensation of the barrel of a revolver against the side of his head.'

'What did he do?'

'He didn't do anything. He just said: "Oh hell! . . . I give up!"'

She feels let down. Surely it couldn't have happened that simply! Her suspicions return, and her face becomes sceptical once more.

'You didn't get hurt?'

'I told you . . .'

Because he is afraid of scaring her! So she remains convinced that he's been in a fight, that he's a hero, that . . .

Her eye catches the tray on the table.

'And then you ground fresh coffee! You had the . . . You thought you would make me coffee and bring me my breakfast . . .'

She knows she is going to cry . . . She cries with tenderness, with admiration . . .

'And you did that for me! Why? Tell me why.'

'Simple! I did it because I hate you! I hate you so much that when Lucas gets here with the taxi, I shall leave and take my turkey with me. Did I mention that the Musician is trussed up like a turkey? I had to borrow the rope from poor old Lapie.'

'And what about me?'

He has great difficulty in not smiling at this 'what-about-me?' into which she has unconsciously put her entire soul.

What about me? Am I to be left here all alone? There won't be anyone left to take me seriously? No one to ask me questions, tease me, no one to . . .

What about me? . . .

'Go and sort yourself out with Jacques. They still sell grapes, oranges and champagne in the shop in the Faubourg Saint-Honoré, which I believe you know. I've forgotten what the visiting hours are at the hospital, but they'll tell you.'

A taxi, a sight so familiar in Paris, looks rather incongruous out here on roads which wind through country fields.

'Better get dressed.'

And while, without turning round, he leaves her and starts going down the stairs, he hears her murmur:

'Why are you always so horrible to me?'

A moment later he is circling the Musician, who is tied up in old Lapie's chair. There is a sound of footsteps coming and going above his head, of splashing water, clothes being taken off hangers in the wardrobe, a shoe which falls on the floor and is picked up, the voice of someone who, in the heat of the moment, cannot stop talking although there's no one there.

Quite. That's Félicie for you!